Ladies in Charge

Arian Mabe

This is a collection of short stories with femdom as a focus. There are a mix of characters, though there are plenty of dominant mares to be found in this collection! Some human characters are included but furry characters are predominant.

The collection includes: oral sex, vaginal sex, anal sex, BDSM, domination/submission play, roleplaying, bondage, pegging, size difference play and foot play.

Table of Contents

The Cherry Wood Stocks

They dominated my dreams, those cherry wood stocks. The old-fashioned kind, they were carved out of the finest wood, painted with a rich varnish. The wood would be curved on top, a smooth design that begged the attention of the eye, but it was not required for them to do their job in securing the head and wrists of their so-called unlucky victim. The courtyard surrounding them was constructed of old stone, as if it was in the grounds of a castle of olden times, something out of the darkest and most twisted fairytale one could possibly dream up. But the stocks themselves were the main focus, set up so that the victim would have to stand bent over at the waist, their humility on show for a very public humiliation. There would be a separate set of stocks to lock up one's ankles too, if needed, but I never got that far in my dream before ejaculating and waking with a start, a sticky, aroused mess of a man. I never felt like very much of a man after those dreams.

I was a man with very specific pleasures and fantasies, as you may well enough be able to tell. Submission... Oh, it was and still is a beautiful thing, something that made my blood sing from the very first moment that I discovered it for myself. I knew that I wanted it as I rose on to the cusp of manhood and, from there, everything just seemed simple to know and much more difficult to take for my own. I could not find myself a partner willing to satisfy those needs, which was perhaps a failing on my part for searching in the wrong circles, and so I remained a bachelor moving through increasingly kinky circles, learning all the way what it meant to be one in my position. I rather liked that position too, beneath the heal of a dominatrix, her eyes hard and passionate with raw power, the flash of pain mingling with the lick of pleasure.

Ah yes... Each and every new experience was something special indeed, just what drove me on and on to search out those pleasures, new experiences the joy of my life while I remained, at least mostly, single. And it was in search of those pleasures, often seen as beneath a businessman of my standing in the world of work and the community, that I met the gryphon called Helena.

It was impossible for the gryphon with scarlet feathers tipped with blue to not catch one's eye, whether they were attracted to anthropomorphic beings or not. It had been difficult for them to integrate, many years back, but so much time around the creatures, demanding acceptance in society at large, allowed them to blend in, slowly and surely. Of course, they still received some rather odd looks, but they knew what corners and pools of society that they fit into best and found their place just like any other minority. There was still work to be done but, for the moment, all beings like them could hope for was one step and one day at a time.

Helena... It was a beautiful name but only a name that I learned later. The very first time I saw her, she was standing over a human male who crawled on the floor, his head lowered as if to shield himself from the rain of blows. Her whip flashed out, a thickly tailed flogger, and he cried, although the spurts of his half-hard cock gave his real game away as pleasure mingled erotically with pain. The music pulsed and throbbed, a driving beat to match the swing of her tool, the gryphon's beak clacking sharply as she spat a cry, a curse – whatever was needed to heat her blood and fuel the fire of the scene to an ever-heightening burn.

A gryphon was a special being indeed, standing taller than most human beings with an avian head and torso. Her beak was as black as the night sky with the faintest hint of blue around the corners of what I would have called lips, but were evidently named something else, her eyes a searing aquamarine that stood out sharply from her crimson feathers. Those feathers stretched all the way down to her toned stomach, visible between the bottom of her corset and her thong, which barely seemed to cover anything at all, feathers blending into similarly shaded fur, so smooth and seamless that the line itself was difficult to discern. Her hind paws were feline in nature, a tail tucked down over the back of the thong that curled up to a fluffy tip. If I didn't know better, I would have said that it was feline-like, but it curled back and forth with so much more flexibility that it was quite clear, even to me, that the gryphon was a creature of fantasy entirely different to anything of our skin-deep realm of humanity and what we thought we knew.

We knew so little. And the wings, of course, served to complete her beautiful body, tucked in close to her back most of the time and, unfortunately, too small to render flight possible in any sense of the word. I asked her, much later, whether she thought she could glide with them and she had laughed so hard that tears rolled down her face. I supposed I could not have been held at fault for curiosity though.

Her eye caught mine as I stood and watched, my lower jaw ever so slightly slack and a drink that I had not yet touched clasped in my trembling left hand. Helena smiled as well as a gryphon could, shoulders pushing back as if she was trying to make herself seem larger and more intimidating than she even was. The truth of it was, however, that she didn't need to do anything at all to seem exactly as dominantly powerful as she was, the lure of it radiating from every last feather on her toned and curved body.

"Are you watching me, little man?"

Reminiscent of how men in the work world so often referred to women (including femfurs, of course) as "little ladies," it sent a shiver down my spine. I wanted to be a little man, just with the right one. And there was something about Helena that made my legs want to buckle right then and there, although I wasn't even thinking about anything to do with my pleasure even at that moment in time.

She had me, my will and whims lost to everything and anything she ever desired of me, as sordid and devious as her mind was. Helena was more than just a gryphon but a cunning being who took every last fantasy I thought I had at the very limits of my psyche and turned me to darker and more twisted means still, pushing my boundaries and taking pleasure from my screams.

I wouldn't have had it any other way.

And she bought me those cherry wood stocks. Our relationship developed, although it was not like any other I had either been in or seen for myself, the dynamic firmly skewed entirely in her favour. I could be the big businessman as much as I wanted at work, but, as soon as I stepped back through the door of her home – she had had me give up my high-floor apartment close to the city centre – everything was back to how it should be. I had to make the money I needed to survive and, of course, provide for her and her needs, but the collar slipping back around my neck was what I needed at the end of a long, mentally gruelling day.

Off came the suit and down I went on my knees, not even knowing that the cherry wood stocks were waiting for me, primed and polished (not by Helena, of course) in one of the several play rooms in her large, expansive home. There were no other houses bordering hers and the gryphon had plenty of space in which to enjoy her income as a dominatrix and every last penny of mine too, although I gave it all to her gladly and with thanks. For I knew as a man who had once had the newest and best of everything that money did not buy happiness, even if it could buy luxury. Helena was my happiness and serving her on my knees would forever secure my place in life and love. I needed nothing more than that.

"Ah, little one," she purred, stepping out from the lounge with a silk robe draped over her shoulders, open at the front. "I wondered when you would return to me."

Half out of the suit, I hurriedly shed my trousers, socks and shoes too, putting them to the side for the moment; I could sort and fold them as needed later. Helena was more important.

No, that was not right: not the right way to speak or think about her. My *mistress* was more important than folding clothes.

I smiled privately to myself, turning my cheek into the curve of her delicate fingers, talons lightly brushing my skin and five o'clock shadow. There. That was better. I could not slip up, regardless of how long a day it had been or of how tired I was. My mistress deserved the best, the very best, and that included the best of me too.

"I have a surprise for you."

That caught my attention, not that it had not already been focused on her. I did not dare speak but I raised my eyebrows curiously, the urge to know flickering through my body like a living force beneath the fragile barrier of my skin. My blood rose for her, cock thickening and plumping out just from the barest suggestion that she had something planned for me, knowing just how her devious mind worked by that point. If there was something in store, well, it was going to be exquisite.

The chain leash clipped to the collar around my throat and I could not help but moan, leaning into it as she led me up the moderately wide, wooden staircase. One step at a time... I could have been ascending either the stairway to heaven or the stairway to my doom, wondering just what was waiting ahead of me. My cock was hard and throbbing regardless, aroused just from being near her as I shifted my weight constantly, the pace too slow and foreboding to settle my anxious mind.

"Come now."

I missed a step, stumbled and tightened the chain. Her wings snapped out as she scowled and I cowered instantly, shrinking back enough to put a little distance between us but not enough to tighten the chain again – not because I didn't want it to pull on my neck again but because I didn't want the surprise to disappear, just because of a misstep. As erotic and delightful as being tied up and beaten to a whimpering, quivering mess was, I desperately wanted to know what she had in store for me. And that meant that I had to be good.

"Keep up, pet."

I trembled. Oh, how I loved when she called me that, for I was nothing more than an obedient pet at her heels, wanting her approval above all else. It was her lead that bolstered my spirits on the worst of days and I stepped forward, keeping my stance low and respectful even as her expression softened and we came to the third door in the upstairs hallway, the carpet there softer beneath my bare feet and knees, as I dropped quickly, than the bare board of the hollow-sounding stairs were. They looked impressive but they would never be as impressive as the towering gryphon standing over me, appearing taller than ever as she unlocked the door with a long, metal key that seemed suited to the grandeur of her abode.

I didn't dare look at her breasts, even as her robe slipped open further and she tugged me commandingly inside. I knew that that may turn away my surprise, render me useless for the night and the surprise, perhaps, taken away forever.

I could not take that risk.

"Eyes down."

She made it easy to obey, my mistress did. The leash dropped and I put my palms flat on the floor, shoulders rounding forward just to keep my position a little lower still, ensuring that I would not be tempted, regardless of what happened, to look up and spoil things. If she had gone to such lengths – all for me! – things had to be very special indeed.

And Helena made it easier still to not look and disobey when she slipped the fleece-padded blindfold over my eyes, the fleece ensuring that I could not see anything, not a single sliver of light slipping in the traitorous edges that could tease and spoil, as they did. I had no choice but to relax into her hold, as much as my heart pounded, and allow her to guide me up on to my feet, not knowing what lay in wait.

"You're so cute in your bare skin..."

Vulnerable was more like it: exposed and vulnerable. But that was just what I wanted to be as my wrists bumped into something solid, easing into curved gaps like half-moons that cradled my unusually slender wrists like a lover's caress. I shifted there, the curved wood cupping them from the underside. Although I had never even felt that type of wood before, something about it made my heart leap as she pushed my head forward too to rest in a like-shaped hollow, my Adam's apple bobbing as I gulped and parted my lips.

Was it... Oh... Oh, it could *not* be!

Against myself, I whimpered as the very solid wood of what could only be a set of stocks closed over my wrists, the click of the locking mechanism impossible to miss. The stocks – were they cherry wood? How could she have known? There was no way, however, for me to see while blindfolded and I was forced to speculate and dream as she made sure I was bent over with my backside raised for any kind of attention that she wished to give it. And I could only imagine that the brand of attention she had in mind for me was particularly wicked indeed.

Just as I'd wanted.

"Little man... You should have known better than to allow yourself to slip into my claws."

I could hear her walking around me, but I did not dare chance speaking, in case it would put the fantasy to rest. But I was right where I wanted to be, in her claws, and she knew that too, Helena knowing every last one of my most private thoughts and what I didn't even know myself too. The gryphon clacked the edges of her beak together lightly as she circled, possibly admiring me from all angles, but the slither of her silk robe slipping to the floor was what set my heart racing the most. If she left the blindfold on, I wouldn't even get to see her bare feathers and the beautiful rise of her breasts, but perhaps that was just what she wanted. And Helena *always* got exactly what she wanted.

Her hands landed on my backside and I groaned as she dug in the sharp points of her fingertips. The claws made it difficult for her to write sometimes but she never would have considered filing them down like some other gryphons, instead keeping them deadly and sharpened to a shocking point. It didn't matter too much in her work as a dominatrix anyway, perhaps even drawing a few more clients to her. None had a relationship with her like I did though, even if she did sometimes have me in the same room while she was working, just to cement my position under her.

But I could not think of that as her hands roamed, squeezing and pinching and digging in wherever they pleased, for she could, in fact, do exactly as she pleased. The gryphon keened softly, the churring sound rising up deep from the back of her throat, and I trembled to hear it, automatically tugging at my restraints and spreading my legs for her, widening my stance.

"What a good boy you are..."

Yes... Yes, I was good – good for her. I would *always* be good for her, especially if she bought me such divine toys. I did not know if there were any toys left in her home that had not yet been used on me, but I only welcomed each and every new one with the gratefulness and thanks that my mistress truly deserved and, of course, commanded. But the toy that she pressed to my backside was a familiar one, slick and cold and dripping with a blessed amount of lubricant: a large dildo that resembled the cock of a male, adult gryphon. It was one layered with divine ridges and nodules that sent my head spinning as it ground up against my prostate, for I had had it shoved into me enough times to know each and every last curve of that cock in intimate detail.

And it seemed that I was about to become privy to it again as she pressed the time to my anal ring, demanding entry that was willingly given. I was well-trained in that department after the vast number of toys in her entire arsenal had been tried on me, one after the other. Why, the gryphon had even sent me to work with a toy shoved up there, just to keep me squirming and stretched for longer, although that had been more uncomfortable than just being fucked with one of her strap-on devices. I moaned and hung my head, trying to brace and failing as my legs scrambled to support me, head spinning and need rising even as my cock throbbed and splattered cold pre-cum.

"Such a needy one... Do you really think I'm going to let you cum?"

Although I knew how to hold myself back, there was a chastity device around too for the times when she did not trust me, even though I knew too that I could orgasm even with that cage locked around my pathetic dick. It never was enough to satisfy Helena, as she had told me on multiple occasions, and a failed, weak orgasm that spent a milky load without sating my need just made me more obedient, sweetly broken more and more with every passing day.

The toy pressed in and I groaned loudly, trying to rock my hips back to ease it in, but she wasn't exactly about to go easy on me either, driving the full length of it up into my forbidden passage. No matter how pleasurable it was to be so deliciously stretched out and full, feeling as if I was going to split open in the most bone-shakingly erotic way, I could not *cum* and I had to be *good* for my mistress above all else.

She worked the toy back and forth inside me, mimicking the thrusts of a male as she took control of the situation, licking the edges of her beak with a lewd, wet smack of saliva. It pounded and drove into me, grinding up against my prostate in a way that made my cock twitch and jump and jerk against my will, pre-cum forced in a milky swathe from the dripping head. There wasn't anything I could do about that, shifting my weight in an effort to keep myself away and the pressure down, although it was shocking just how swiftly the need to climax rose in the back of my mind.

No... No, I could not think of that. I moaned and rolled my head within the confines of the stocks, the erotic feel of the wood on my skin enough to draw another groan from me and then another. Did she know just what she was doing, trapping me as she did? She knew... Of course, she knew. There was little any man in my position, of my subtle inclinations, could do to hold back climax even as she chuckled throatily, the pace of the toy picking up as she controlled and drove it deep into my most intimate of holes.

"Don't you dare cum, pet..."

Oh, it was such a taunt, for she knew just what she was doing and how long she had kept me denied. I only was ever allowed to ejaculate under her control and that was rare enough as it was. Ever on edge when I was around her, I hissed and clenched my teeth, striving and failing to think of anything else at all to distract myself, the feel of her hands on me stimulation enough to get me hot and randy and wound up in all the best kind of ways.

But it was the worst too when she had told me to hold back and I could not help but brace for that cock, grunting like a wild animal myself as I tried to hold back, the jerk and twitch of my cock almost shameful. I was not in control of my own body, and, in all honesty, I hadn't been for a very long time, which was just the way she liked it.

Of course, she orchestrated the whole thing so that I was set up to fail, but that didn't stop me from trying all the same, only wanting to please her even as my need to cum rose and rose. There was only so much I can do as those ridges popped over my prostate and I hissed through my teeth, slamming my neck into the stocks furiously – yet even that pain could not prevent orgasm from spilling hastily over the edge in a cruelly stolen climax that should not have been my own to take.

Helena clucked her tongue, disappointment evident, but I was lost to orgasm, balls churning to spill my load, a pitifully small amount considering the amount of time I'd been so denied, over the floor beneath me. I could not see how much it was, however, and neither did I care, groaning and grunting and rocking my hips as my body coaxed every last bit of pleasure out that it could while that dildo stilled inside me, Helena stepping back and away.

And that was just when I knew that everything was very, very wrong. My breath caught in my throat even as I gasped and heaved and tried to catch it again, lungs aching and head spinning in the darkness of my world, every other sensation heightened, including the feel of her hands, which had been noticeably taken from me. There was no telling what would come next, although I was hardly in a position to complain or even go against what she wanted, trapped and wanton and still craving more with every lengthy moment that passed.

If there'd been a clock in that play room, its ticking would have driven me mad, waiting and waiting and waiting while my anal passage squeezed around the shaft in my backside. If I released it, I could only imagine what worse fate would befall me than what was already in store, my heart beat drumming sickeningly against my eardrums.

"Little pet... I think you know that you did wrong there."

Oh, how I knew and I groaned and closed my eyes even as she ripped off the blindfold, revealing my fate to me in the form of that accursed cock-cage that both made my heart leap and plummet, conversely, at the same time. My softening cock was unceremoniously stuffed into it and I moaned, trying to pull away and rattling the stocks, although Helena knew, of course, that I wasn't going anywhere.

The cage slipped over and locked tightly, a ring looped around my balls too to keep them separate from my shaft, which looked as if it was in prison with a ring of bars covering it, the tip still glistening and leaking as if it still thought that it would get to enjoy itself again. Ah, if only my body knew what came of disobeying, even if it was oh so very sweet in the erotic heat of the moment. I'd both regret and relish that moment of pleasure for months to come as she tormented and tortured me just as I craved to be.

But when she lifted a paddle formed of sleek, shiny wood, I gulped and hung my head submissively, cock trying to harden again against the limits of the cage. It could go nowhere, of course, but it still wanted to climax and feel that pleasure, my body and mind seeming to be separate beings as she controlled me. And maybe Helena had the divine power to separate the two also: there was no way for me to tell as I was just her human pet, there to obey and serve.

"One-hundred strikes should do it."

I tensed for the first and howled, fingers opening and closing frantically as my body tried to swing away from the stinging slap, which struck my backside seemingly with all of the power in her arm. And that was considerable considering her size, the gryphon screeching with her wings flared, eyes narrowed and blazing with the control she held over me. If I'd ever had any doubt whatsoever over how much she loved me and lusted after me, even as her submissive pet, it was clear in the slickness of her pussy, the soft, pink lips glistening with that arousal even as the aroma of her need hung heavily in the air between us.

And, so, I bore through each and every strike she made, the slap of the paddle ringing through the play room as she pounded me, leaving the dildo wedged into my backside as another reminder of just how small and weak I was in comparison to her. She controlled me – she *sodomised* me. Just how much of a man did that make me? But I could not have been a man and been with her, my stunning mistress, and so I chose being less and less of a man each and every day, bending the knee to my dominant mistress for the shared pleasure we rejoiced in on either end of the spectrum.

It was worse when she swapped to a cane, the flat side of the paddle able to spread the load of the strikes more evenly. There was no escaping from a cane, however, which swiftly layered my backside in red line after line – not that I could twist around to see that, of course. I knew it in just how furiously the tears rolled down my cheeks, although I would not have changed anything for the world, for I was in the place I needed to be before my mistress and any punishment she doled out would be as fair and just as she was.

Fifty-five... Fifty-six... Fifty-seven...

I howled and threw my weight into the stocks, instinct taking over as she hooked a hand around my hip, dragging me back without care or mercy to finish the job that she'd begun.

Sixty-nine... Seventy... Seventy-one...

I barely noticed when the cane was swapped for a somewhat gentler riding crop, although there was nothing gentle about it on skin that was bruised and reddened, searing through with heat. There would no doubt be welts on my backside come the next morning, but they would be cared for and soothed only once my punishment was over. And I continued to count each and every stroke even as I panted and whined and whimpered as if I did not have the capability of speech, my muscles trembling so badly that it was a wonder that I was even able to keep my buttocks raised for my mistress' strokes.

I'd never before been so glad to count the final blow, collapsing weakly and hanging from the stocks, my cock completely flaccid despite the rampant arousal coursing through me. If I'd cum during the course of the beating, I had not noticed, pain overruling any pleasure that my body may have wanted to feel. I could try to please myself, of course, after the fact, but there was no way I was getting off without severe stimulus with the cage locked around my shaft, no matter how many moans passed the sacred barrier of my lips.

Helena smirked, tipping her head to the side as she forced my chin up to her, eyes alight with mischief.

"There you are, little man... Now, does that not feel better? You shall not disobey me again."

Although what my body did when pushed to that edge was beyond my control, I would do everything in my power to obey and, really, that was all I could do. If things went wrong...well, the punishment wasn't that bad and I could already feel my need rising once again, hips lifting despite my exhaustion to present myself with that dildo stretching my backside wide. It would undoubtedly gape lewdly when the toy was removed, but the control of that too was in my mistress' hands and hers alone.

Regardless of how long the cage stayed on, I was hers to do with just as she pleased. And that was the true pleasure beauty of being her loyal submissive. I didn't have to think and I most certainly didn't have to be anything that I wasn't, not when I was locked in the cherry wood stocks, the smooth wood slick in places with my sweat and a little spittle too that could not be helped. It was beautiful, the very best surprise she ever could have given me – at least, until the next one and the next one, Helena never failing to surprise me.

I would always be hers.

Pony Play

The werewolf squirmed in his bondage, on his knees in one of the stalls of an indoor barn that should have held horses if not for the fact that they had been ushered out in the snow for the day. It did not matter to them that it was cold and flakes of snow still fell outside, their winter coats thick and fluffed up to keep any moisture on the outside of their coats, the under layer still warm and dry. They were a tougher sort than most anthros who bundled themselves up in layer upon layer of clothing that probably didn't do all that great of a job of keeping the cold out, based on the quality those days.

Yes, it was cold, but not so cold that Arnou was shivering, grunting and pressing his tongue up against the bit in his mouth, holding his jaws apart where it could not slide into a gap between his teeth like it would in the mouth of a stallion anthro. With a moan, he wiggled his tongue more insistently against the bit, saliva drooling but in an erotic kind of way. He could go for a stallion right there where he was, his tail lifted and he was sure that his tail hole could be accessed too, for there was one very good reason that he was not cold in the barn.

A latex suit, after all, was something that would very much keep an anthro warm, much less a werewolf with such a thick coat of fur that it was a wonder that he'd even been able to struggle into the get-up to begin with. Rose had been particularly ruthless in getting him into it – why did he keep drinking with her again after that party? It hadn't led to anything happening at the point of drinking this time, of course, but it had let slip a promise that he would help out in her barn one day the following week and, being a wolf of his word, Arnou had turned up bright and early with the sleep barely rubbed from his eyes. He just hadn't known that what the wicked red mare had meant was that he would be put to work in a very different way than he imagined.

The latex suit sucked in around his limbs, so perfectly fitted that it was a wonder that it had not been custom made for him. A flexible suit, it would not have restricted his movement if he had been free to move, but it was patterned to look like the hide of a black equine with a white rump, speckled over that white with black splotches.

Rose had giggled and slapped that white patch, making his backside clench up pleasurably in anticipation of what was to come, saying that he was an Appaloosa, whatever that meant. He wasn't all that clued up on what went on in the equine world and he didn't need to be either to enjoy every last bit of whatever it was that she had in mind for him.

The suit was just the start of it, however, sleek latex running down his legs to a pair of hoof boots that hid his naturally large paws from view. The anatomy of his legs would have set him up well to walk in them, pushed up on to his toes, if he'd been free to do so. For the harness encasing his torso, straps even reaching down and around his thighs, made sure that he was locked in place and unable to enjoy that bare minimalist freedom of movement. He clinked and jingled with a multitude of O-rings, but the restrictive nature of the mask set around his head did not really allow him enough flexibility to look down and admire his own body. Although his sheath was tucked away in a fold of latex, enough space for his balls to be cradled comfortably too, there was the possibility of it growing and slipping into view at any time, which was good. It wasn't a time that he wanted to be denied, as submissive at heart as he was.

The mask though, oh...that was the final piece, the piece that made his heart pound and tongue try to loll from his muzzle, pushing against that bit. A full pony play mask, it turned him into a latex equine, the head larger and blockier than his own as if he was a Spanish stallion set up for a parade. A cascade of horse hair fell luxuriously down the back of his neck and it was all he could do to resist tossing it, the urge to prance near enough overwhelming as he snorted through the curved nostril breathing holes in the mask, nose moist against the interior. He could see just about through the eye holes too, although his range of vision was severely limited by a set of blinkers attached to the bridle that had gone on over the mask, bit clanking obnoxiously against his teeth as he tried to open his mouth.

A fake horse tail hung down over his own, hiding it from view, but he could not feel it lying against the backs of his thighs as he wriggled and pulled at the leather straps that kept him tethered to the wall, hooked into the harness, perhaps, at some point across his back. Arnou had not seen that bondage being connected and knew no more than that, his paws slipped into huge hooves that covered his paws up to the wrists, denying the use of his fingers even as he growled and champed eagerly at the bit, upper arms locked in against his torso, so that he could use his forearms only. Not that that would have done him any good, of course, with a spreader bar between his knees anyway, but the restrictive nature of his situation just made him want to be right there, where he was, on his knees all the more, moaning and trying not to let his cock throb out full and hard too soon. If there was one part of him that he didn't want to get cold, it was that!

But the wolf was not destined to be left all out on his lonesome for too much longer, although it was not quite the equine that he expected who returned in a sharp clip-clop of hooves down the centre aisle. Arnou caught his breath, ears trying to prick and swivel, folded into the shape of the latex horse ears of the mask itself, but could not see out of the straw-lined stable, the wooden door across the aisle not offering any more idea of what was to come than what his lust-addled mind could cook up for itself.

What would she do to him? Arnou daydreamed as those hooves drew closer, light and ringing as if they wanted their presence to be known and heard ahead of time. Perhaps the strap-on again... Oh, she'd had such a good collection of dildos to use on him, his hole hadn't felt the same for a week! Who cared about such things like sitting down comfortably when they could be fucked so hard and repeatedly, moaning out their pleasure over and over again after all?

Groaning, the wolf tried to roll his head from one shoulder to the other, shivering in the confines of the suit, the very tip of his red shaft poking from the latex sheath. No! He had to think of something else, anything else. He just needed to calm down a bit and *not* spill his load right there and then, steady his breathing, think sensible thoughts, *non*-sexy thoughts.

"My, my, my... Now, aren't you a cutie?"

Arnou jumped and would have wagged his tail to be so addressed – hey, he was pretty cute, he had to say – but the base was too tightly trapped in latex, forced through a hole that had been cut for the natural tail of an anthro without forcing it down against their rump, forming an unsightly shape. The hair of the false equine tail shivered a little, however, paying homage to the play he'd volunteered for, although he had not quite expected to be trussed up and bound in a stall, waiting on her attention.

She was a bay mare – he knew that term, after some lecturing – with a coat of brown hair and black stockings on her bare legs, something about the fact that she was dressed in jean-shorts on such a cold, snowy day telling a tale that she'd been expecting him. Why else would she be dressed so skimpily as he rolled his head, trying to get a glimpse of just what lay higher up but all he could see was a crop-top tied below what he hoped was a very lovely pair of breasts. Hey, a werewolf could only hope!

"Such a fine pony," she murmured, dropping a tangle of leather strapping beside him. "Are you all lonely here? I'm sure you are! You wouldn't mind the company of lil' ol' me now, would you?"

She put the drawl on thickly and tipped his head up to hers, a pair of brilliant blue eyes locking on to his, a mealy muzzle with lips quirking up cutely at the corners filling his line of sight. Arnou whimpered and moaned within the mask, although the sound came out muffled even as he sought to make himself heard, the wolf but a toy to be used as the mare commanded. And she had big plans for him indeed.

"Hey, Sal, get your tail over here!" She trilled, meeting his eyes as he swung his head to face her, blinkers framing the edges of his vision. "We've got a newbie here for a little company..."

Sal? Who was Sal? And who was she?

"Jessie? What's going on here? You know I'm busy. Oh... *Oh.* I see now!"

The stallion loomed over the mare, thus named as Jessie, a hand braced on the frame of the doorway, lips pulled up in a smile that perhaps didn't promise what Arnou may have expected. And, oh, the stallion was divine, dressed more appropriately for the weather in jeans and boots and a coat that was swiftly shed from a shirt-clad chest and bare forearms rippling with muscle. Arnou couldn't hold himself back as the stud himself slipped his shirt off too, revealing a broad chest that was simply desperate for the lap of a tongue, his palomino coat golden and shining radiantly even beneath the overhead lighting strips which, to be fair, were perhaps not the most flattering at the best of times as they buzzed away.

"A fine new filly, I see, for the barn... You'll do well here, if you behave yourself and are trainable. Quite a big filly though, you are...aren't you?"

"Mmmph...nnnfff..."

Arnou grunted against the gag, cursing his lack of speech even as he submissively tried to tuck his tail down, ears folding back within the suit. He wasn't a filly! But, oh, he'd be a filly any day for that stallion, his heart pounding and blood pumping harder than ever as Sal pressed his lips to the latex ones of the suit and forced his tongue aside.

The werewolf could not have honestly said that he'd never been kissed in such a mask before, but the sensation was purely exotic as his mouth was dominated, the wolf barely able to use his eager tongue, in turn, to kiss the equine back as his head was forcibly held in place. Arnou wasn't about to go anywhere, however, not even with the bondage ensuring that that was well and truly out of the question, his cock hard and throbbing and the tip glistening with an alluring bead of pre-cum.

"He's ready," she whispered huskily, slipping her tongue back out to play it across that finger as if she thought she might just have missed a taste on the digit. "So ready... Rose really does find the best toys for us. How lucky are we?"

Sal rolled his eyes and snorted heavily, flicking his white forelock out of his eyes as he unlocked Arnou's bonds from the wall of the stable; he wouldn't need to be secured in place for what he had in mind.

"You call it luck... I consider it a work bonus."

Jessie giggled and darted out of the stable as Sal took control, gripping the back of the harness and grunting as he hefted up the werewolf's weight. He was not a light load, although it was mostly muscle beneath the thick, fluffy coat of fur, and neither was the stallion built like one of the draft types, able to haul truly magnificent loads. Sal managed well enough, however, and Arnou's vision swung about to show the centre aisle of the barn, the doors open just a little at the far end to look out on to the snow-covered fields and Jessie flashing across his line of sight with a bale of straw hefted up with two hands.

"Oof!"

She grunted as she dropped it just in time for Sal to plop the wolf on to it, the pony-boi tipping forward as his nose threatened to smush itself right into the straw. But the stallion was there to hold him up, controlling the situation even as Arnou wriggled, just to feel and enjoy how helpless he was. It was hardly as if he would have needed the bondage to enjoy just what any stallion had in store for him, if he was honest, but it just added that exquisite little edge when he thought he didn't have a say, that he couldn't get out if he wanted to and was just a toy for them to pass around and use as they willed.

The stallion grunted and eased down the zip of his jeans, Arnou's eyes locking on to that bulge in intricate detail as he held his breath. Balanced on his knees as Sal supported him, he could have tipped forward or off the straw bale at any moment, although he wasn't thinking of that in the heat of the moment. No, all he was thinking about was getting that glorious hunk of stallion-meat into his muzzle, tongue pushing anxiously against the bit as it was revealed, a mottled pink and grey shaft firming up hard and proud before his muzzle.

Whining, the wolf clamoured for it, twisting and bucking his hips to no avail, his own shaft drooling a near clear string of pre-cum. If he'd been free, he simply wouldn't have been able to hold himself back but, as it was, he could not even get the bit out from between his teeth to free up his jaws for that cock.

"Aw, let me, pony, I got you..."

And then Jessie's hands were there, somehow knowing which buckles had to be undone to free that bit from his mouth, although he almost lamented its absence after the cold metal of a snaffle had warmed up to his mouth. He groaned as he was relieved from it, barely taking a moment in which to work his jaw as Sal hooked his thumb into the corner of his mouth, tucked into the side of the mask, and forced him to yield, that cock looming closer and closer.

"Open wide."

He would have taken the cock into his mouth of his own free will but then Sal's hands were gone, his cock shoved between the latex lips of the mask and past the very soft and real ones of Arnou, the werewolf moaning luxuriously around that fat cock as it disappeared right up into the back of his throat. His gag reflex kicked in, causing his chest to convulse even if the bulk of his body could not afford such a range of motion, the werewolf forcing himself to relax as the stallion re-set himself and found a better angle.

"Better take it all, pony, or they're going to have to put you through more training..."

Oh, but he wouldn't have minded more training – not if it involved that cock! It slid down over his tongue, hard and spurting already, and he groaned around it, gulping reflexively to ensure that he could take as much as possible. His wolf-like muzzle was long enough to take most with ease but it was the fatter base past the throb of the medial ring that was the most difficult, Arnou grunting as he tried to push his head down, supported solely, for the moment, by that fat cock alone.

"Such a little cock-hungry pony," Sal mocked him, running his hands down Arnou's back as if to toy with the harness, the latex suit defining his muscle clearly. "You needed this, didn't you? That's why you were waiting there for us, all gagged and bound and pretty in your suit?"

Of course, Arnou could not answer but he didn't have to answer when the stud stallion was there to take him as he pleased, holding the wolf up to ram into his mouth, fucking it as if it was just another hole to be filled. And the wolf languished in the feeling of being reduced to that, allowing the equine to use him as he willed and only pressing his tongue up to the underside of that cock, vision filled with a golden, ripped stomach and muscle on muscle that seemed to go on and on. He may not have been a draft horse, but the stallion was packing, for sure, and his cock was crammed into the very best place it could have possibly found, a wet and warm muzzle welcoming him in as Arnou pressed his tongue up to the underside, content to simply be used even as his own hard shaft was left completely and utterly unaddressed.

Set further back from the scene, however, was a certain chestnut mare watching from the hayloft, arms folded and her eyebrows raised. Unbeknownst to those who had fallen, so sweetly, into her little trap, she leaned back comfortably, watching the charge that she'd brought into the stables be enjoyed as only a good pony should. And he had not yet earned that right.

"Well, well, well," Rose murmured to herself, drumming her fingers across her bare forearm as she leaned back against a small rectangle of hay, ready to be tossed down into one of the waiting stalls. "Who knew that a wolf could be so easily swayed into the pony ways?"

Of course, it was not as if Arnou had been given much choice or say in the matter as she licked her lips and merely enjoyed the show, a whip loosely held in one of her hands. It was a fine whip too, a schooling whip with a little extra reach on it than either a jumping or a standard riding crop. Most liked the schooling whip because it let them touch the hindquarters of their mount without taking their hands off the reins. She didn't use it like that on a feral or on an anthro, however, gentler with those of the four-legged kind than she was of the two-legged pony bois in her stable.

Running her fingers down the leather to the tassel at the tip, she inhaled slowly and deeply, groaning faintly as he took that stallion's cock straight down his throat, helpless to resist and, truly in the set of his body, not seeming to *want* to resist either. Ever the voyeur, she watched and licked her lips, a hand slipping between her thighs as she let the scene she'd set up play out before her, Jessie grinding up against Arnou's backside as if she too believed herself a stallion best suited to mounting and fucking him good and hard. The chestnut mare drew in a breath, nostrils fluttering as her eyes hardened, lips pulling up on just the one side into a devious smirk.

That newest pony needed a taste of that whip.

There was no stopping the course of action even as she slowly made her way down from the hayloft, taking her time as she knew that they would be waiting for her right where they were. It did not matter that Jessie had her jean-shorts off and was looking to get next go; the mare herself was not quite dominant enough in heart to take control, even though she had been the one to find Arnou first, which had been her plan. And Sal, of course, was not to be stopped as he grunted and huffed and slammed into the wolf's muzzle, taking his pleasure forcibly from a willing mouth.

Arnou groaned around him, ignorant to the fact that at least the first part of his play was about to come to an abrupt stop, bare hooves ringing out hollowly on the steps down from the hayloft. No one cared and no one had the sense of mind to pause and think as Jessie found the opening in the back of his suit, just beneath his tail, and teased a finger into his anal passage without even the help of any lube. His lust and the fact that she was so very gentle with him eased its passage at least a little, however, Arnou even trying to roll his hips back at her as the stallion ramped up urgently.

"Fuck," he swore, holding Arnou's head firmly in place as he rammed into the full length of his muzzle, the latex nose of the mask nearly pressed up into his crotch – but not quite. "I'm gonna..."

But everyone knew what that utterance meant without needing to complete it and the stallion spent himself into the wolf's muzzle, the werewolf swallowing rapidly just to keep up with him. That thought, however, even though it was one of self-preservation and not wanting to drown in a stream of cum, was forced from even his mind as orgasm washed over him, the sheer eroticism and helplessness of being taken forcing him over the edge right then and there. The finger, joined by a second, penetrating his ass sweetly and curling up against his prostate could have had something to do with it too but Arnou wasn't thinking about that as he tried to howl out his ecstasy around the fat hunk of stallion-meat holding his mouth open.

Climax had never torn through him quite like that before and the werewolf twisted as he tried to free himself, muscles aching viciously as he came up short against the bondage, sweating and whimpering and a mess of a wolf driven to the very brink of submission. Just how low could he go with that cock jammed down his throat, a stud of a stallion huffing above him and a mare eager to use him too, the scent of her pussy thick in the air even with the latex covering his nose. Oh, there was so much more left to come and, as it was, the werewolf did not even soften, shockingly, at the peak of his climax, the tapered length throbbing as if he had not ejaculated in the first place. No, Arnou was ready to be used over and over again just as a good, submissive pony boi always should be…

"I see you've been enjoying yourselves."

That kind of icy tone would have stopped anyone in their tracks, the stallion and mare freezing as their employer's voice cut clear through the air. Arnou, of course, was too busy panting in the blissful afterglow, the splatter of semen on the straw bale impossible to miss as he lay in the line of fire. Even Sal's sheepish withdrawal from his muzzle could not come at a less opportune moment, the wet slide of his shaft as it flopped out, slightly softening, a lewdly erotic sound in the silence that stretched between them.

The whip in Rose's hand could not be ignored, the mare bracing her hooves apart as she played the leather from one hand to the other, eyes hard even as she smirked.

"So…had some fun now, did we?"

"Rose!" Jessie blurted, hands flying to her lips as she pressed her thighs together. "We didn't mean… Oh no! I just saw him there and…"

But the mare didn't really have anything to say and any straws that she was clutching at flew away in the wind, leaving her scrabbling and scraping for anything to say at all. As always, however, yet another came up short and wanting when faced with her potential wrath. They weren't to know that she'd set them all up to come together with the newest stable hand that she'd recruited, even if Arnou was not to be taking on really any traditional stable duties, oh no. Rose had some very special plans for him...

"I'll be taking my newest pony back now," Rose said coolly, making even Sal step back and scuff his hoof across the floor despite his greater height. "Sal. Bring him."

Jessie flapped her hands about, eyes wide and wild as her black mane flew back from her neck, sticking up in all directions as she made as if to lunge, although the mare didn't truly know what she was trying to do at all.

"Ma'am, we didn't mean —"

"Quiet."

And she didn't need to say any more than that, nodding to Sal who grunted and hefted up Arnou in his arms, seeming to struggle an awful lot more with the awkwardly shaped load — at least, when it came to carrying — than he had the first time around. His hooves clopped and scraped noisily as he was thrown off balance and Arnou grunted, held in those tight arms with his cock still half protruding from his latex sheath. Well...he surely wasn't to blame for anything, was he? The wolf groaned and grunted as he was jostled, although he knew that he had no say in anything that came to him, just a pony, as she'd said, in her stable to be used and abused.

Or perhaps that was his own mind putting additional kink on to what he expected of her, the werewolf's kinky mind running amok as he was carried through the barn to a connected indoor arena. The sand packed down and muffled the equine hooves, the newest pony trying his best to nicker as his excitement grew. It seemed like nothing he did or thought of got his cock to soften again and it was all too easy to give in to that submissive impulse inside too, the one that wanted him to quail and whimper and do everything, absolutely everything, he possibly could to please. For it was in his nature and, despite his size, being carried about made him feel like he was so small and insignificant that he would have hunkered right down to the sand and adoringly kissed the hooves of any equine standing before him.

"Here."

Rose pointed with the whip and Sal groaned as he got Arnou into position, setting him so that he was kneeling once more with his shins flat on the floor. Throughout everything, the harness and spreader bar had remained in place, not needing to be removed for him to be used as they please, but Rose had more in mind for the newest pony who very much needed to be taught a lesson in the best way possible.

"Unlock those." She nodded at the spreader bar, her intent obvious. "They won't be needed. The elbows too."

It wasn't as if she'd do the dirty work, after all, when she had the mare and the stallion there to do it for her. Sal and Jessie rushed to obey and helped too to get the sore and stiff Arnou back to his hooves under Rose's critical direction and eye. Standing with his legs trembling from being bound for so long, Arnou was finally able to get a good look at her – his first since actually being put into the bondage by her. And what he saw took his breath away.

Dressed from head to toe in sharp competition gear, she could have been heading out on the show circuit with a pair of cream jodhpurs setting off the hue of her chestnut coat. A black jacket with gleaming buttons completed the ensemble with a white blouse protruding from the neck, the collar crisply pressed – although she had had her pets do that for her, not wanting to waste time on such work. Everything about her screamed control, right down to the line of round plaits lining her neck, drawing attention to the crest, her tail plaited up with what would usually be considered the stray hairs on either side of the dock. Her hooves had been left bare but that was by the by as she strode up to him, popping the tip of the whip beneath his chin, forcing his head up.

"Close your mouth, pony. You're drooling."

How did she know? Did the mask show more than he realised? Arnou snapped his jaws closed again and growled an apology, chin tipped submissively down to his chest as he balanced on one hoof, jigging the other in the air just above the sand. It was not the most comfortable of positions, but Rose cracked a smile and he did it again, waving the hoof as if he was a four-legged equine trying to get her attention without the aid of words, although he was far from impatient, merely waiting on her will and direction.

"You need some training. So, walk on!"

And then that whip flashed down, striking his hip and, without thinking, Arnou yelped and moved forward, clunky and slow in the oversized hoof boots. But that seemed to be just what she wanted as she clucked encouragement to him, walking alongside as she directed him with taps and slaps of the whip. The suit dulled the sensation a little but not enough as she was quick to discipline and correct, guiding him around the outside track and the wooden kickboards topped with letters. As a forty by sixty-metre arena, there was plenty of room to go around and Arnou heaved and puffed for breath, warming up quickly despite the chill in the air. It would have possibly helped some if his cock was not half-hard and slick with his own cum, the inside of that latex sheath more alluringly slippery than he would have liked. But something about doing as she bid settled his mind, easing all worry from it as he concentrated on her tasks and her instructions alone. Why, even the pain blurred into the background of a submissive haze as Rose took hold of the bridle and he leaned, without thinking about what he was doing, into her touch.

Just what did that mare do to him?

"Who took this bit out? Sal. Bring it."

The stallion disappeared as she clucked Arnou into a trot, the werewolf struggling along as he got the hang of how he was supposed to move, slipping more and more into his submissive role of merely being a pony. And, being a pony, he didn't have to think or worry, the ultimate bliss in relaxing into the submissive nuances of what he so loved the most.

In a daze, he moaned and parted his lips within the confines of the mask for that bit, although it was a heavier, chunkier one with a straighter bar that lay across his tongue, not the jointed one of before. But that didn't matter as she secured it in place and tugged the metal up into the corners of his mouth, more easily directing his head.

"Hooves high now – up! Up! *Up!*"

She punctuated each "up" with a tap of the whip on his hooves, forcing him to lift them higher and find his balance until he was doing a pretty good imitation of a Spanish walk, Rose only stepping back when she was good and satisfied to send him on and off in trot. That was much harder work than merely walking but the submissive slip of his mind would not allow him to stop and ask if that was really something she wanted him to do, too far gone and puffing along in an effort to please her.

"There... You're learning. Come in now. To me."

Another command and one that his hooves were moving to complete before his mind actually caught up with what he was doing. He turned in to her and trotted up, light on his hooves and well and truly in the mind of a pony. Play? What was that? The wolf leaned into her touch, rumbling his best impression of a nicker.

"Good pony... I think you're ready."

And then she had hold of the bit, bending him over at the waist as she clucked to Sal, her stable hand moving as obediently as ever to please her whim. It was not as if she was asking him, after all, to do anything all that terrible, grinding up against Arnou's latex-clad buttocks as his cock hardened again into that thick and hefty pole that made him drool so wantonly. He would have done everything to get that shaft back inside him, but it seemed that it was all part of the lesson he was being taught as Rose supported his torso just long enough for Sal to find the slit in the latex underneath the fall of Arnou's horse-hair tail...

"Make sure he feels every inch."

The wolf squealed and stomped, lurching forward against her as that lubed-up cock – thank heavens for lube! – slammed into him, forcing entry and assuming, of course, that it would be given. The surprise, however, just made him clench up around that meaty pole, a thick length of horse-meat that speared into him, taking no prisoners. Deeper and deeper, up past the medial ring: Arnou chomped at the bit, hard on his teeth, and rolled his eyes back into his skull. His cock was already hard and throbbing and it would not be long at all before he was forced into a rude climax, his own weak need getting them better of him, surrounded by powerful equines and simply lusting after everything they had to offer him.

Or was it what he had to offer them? Arnou shook his head, groaning and rolling his hips weakly, clasped between two bodies that would not release him

– not that he wanted to be released. He could not stop himself, body rising and flooding full of heat until he could not help but cum, keening out shrilly and shakily trying to stomp as he spilt his load out over the sand, just barely missing Rose's hooves. He could only *imagine* what would happen if he hit those, black with hoof oil and shiny despite the grains of sand clinging to the toe.

"What a poor little one," she crooned. "You're not getting off with just one climax now, pony."

And it didn't matter to them that he was sensitive, the stallion grabbing his hips under her direction, naked from head to toe with his coat glowing as he fucked the wolf hard and deep. As ordered, he spared not a single inch of his cock as he slammed into the wolf, each thrust of that huge cock grinding up over his prostate and making his head spin and spin and spin. Just how much could a pony take? It remained to be seen as Rose patted his head condescendingly, knowing that he would obey and submit, just as he had before. It was, after all, the wolf's way and it only helped that he was in a jingling harness that reminded him of his place, that whip cracking out across Sal's backside to spur him on, his driving, pounding thrusts increasing swiftly in speed and intensity.

He couldn't take it, howling as he was forced over the edge into another orgasm that hurt as much as it gave him pleasure, mind reeling. Could he take another? Oh, there was no choice in the matter, a submissive pony boy tonguing the bit in his mouth as he groaned and supported himself, bent over with his rump wantonly thrust back for a stallion's attention. But it was the submissiveness his craved, mind swimming pleasantly as he drifted, his anal passage squeezing down on that cock as if his own body was as eager as his mind was to milk that shaft for every drop of cum he had.

The stallion could not go forever, however, which was, most likely, a blessing in disguise as he heaved for breath and slammed into Arnou, eyes rolling with an edge of white as he hastily looked to the mare in charge for permission to do what he so badly craved. But, despite being put in an awkward situation, he was not the one who had to hold back and Rose struck his backside sharply with the crop at the same time as she gave her nod of approval, letting Sal's whinny ring through the arena as his cock pumped and spurted a heavy load of cum deep up under the pony boi's tail.

Lust... Oh, more, he wanted more! Arnou whimpered and moaned, grinding back as much as possible, trusting Sal to support him as his head spun pleasantly, drifting on a current of submissive pleasure from which he wanted no escape. He was right where he wanted to be and he even yipped sadly, breaking from his pony persona, when Sal, finally, had to pull out, that thick shaft sliding messily from his backside, his anal ring more than a little sore from such a pounding. That soreness was something that would, however, only come to light when he came out of sub-space under the hold of a gentle, chestnut hand and a cup of tea ready and waiting for him later on.

He lay back on the sand, guided there, and moaned as his chin was raised, perfectly poised with his tongue sticking out under the bit for something more. Smirking, Rose squeezed his cheeks in, forcing that tongue out even further as she cooed to her new favourite pony.

"I think you wanted some pleasure, did you not, Jessie?"

Rose raised an eyebrow at the bay mare who was still topless, thighs pressed together as she shivered and tried to cover her modesty in the cool of the indoor arena.

"Um, yes, ma'am, but I didn't know –"

"Come here."

Whimpering and whining, she hobbled over to the owner of the barn, eyes downcast even if the hard perk of her nipples betrayed that she had wanted it all along too. Jessie was not a mare to hide her feelings and allowed herself to be borne down to the sand, sitting astride his raised muzzle with her dripping pussy on view for all that bore witness to her lust. Grey skin gave way to pink, fleshy folds past the outer lips, the mare spreading herself for her onlookers, although she only had eyes for Arnou, jigging a hoof as he champed, quite literally, at the bit.

"Hold on," she whispered, eyes sharp with mischief. "You're not properly prepared for a pony boi..."

And then, the finale of it: a carrot. So innocuous and yet impossible to resist for the sense of rampant kink when shoved into just the right hole. Jessie squealed as it was driven up into her pussy, tongue hanging lustfully over her lips as she rolled her eyes back, wanting the pleasure even as she was so swiftly and crudely penetrated.

"Ohhh..."

"Take your treat, pony."

And he did – in more ways than one. Grunting, he worked the carrot from Jessie's pussy with single-minded determination, although the crunch of it disappeared in but a moment; he was more interested in another treat and a prize. Digging his tongue deep into her sex, he lost himself once again in sub-space, barely aware of what he was doing even as he followed direction. More tongue there, deeper now: he was not even in control of the act of giving Jessie oral as she whinnied and trembled, thighs shaking from the sheer strain of staying in such a deep squat for so long.

But it wasn't an option at all to ease herself out of it, Rose's heavy hand on her shoulder bearing her down and down and down until a slutty squeal tore from her throat and she squirted her orgasm over his muzzle, some sliding down and gleaming over the latex mask and more still soaking the fur of his actual wolfen muzzle. Through it all, he played his part, caught up in the role as he sought to please, even though it was the mare commanding the scene who was truly in control, playing their strings like a puppet master.

Licking her juices off his lips, the wolf grunting and shuddered, aching for release despite the strain in his crotch, his body trying to tell him that he needed a break even as he yearned to do more, to be more for the red mare who held his reins in hand. That lesson was complete, the werewolf still needy, but there was so very much more left to learn as his cock twitched and throbbed, Rose chuckling quietly as she traced just the very tip of her finger up the length. Arnou groaned and rocked into her hand, body beyond the control of his mind, a little submissive pony that was good and broken in the very best of ways.

"Don't worry, pony," Rose said, straightening up with the crop tapping the palm of her other hand. "I'm not done with you yet. We have a lot of training to cover, after all, before you'll be ready to service the equine clients of my barn."

The funny thing was that the thought of that didn't fill him with a sense of exhaustion at all. It all sounded rather nice, actually. Very nice. Just what he needed, what he wanted, to adore his superior and do her bidding at all times. He rolled his head from one shoulder to the other, shaky but not worn out, Sal standing to attention with a hard cock that was already being lubed up again by the seductive stroke of a mare's hand.

Arnou groaned, playing with the bit.

The newest pony boi was fit for his job.

Her Gym, Her Rules

The clatter of weights on the gym floor had quieted for a moment at the tail end of the day, the after-work rush having settled to the usual regulars there to work it out one way or another, whether they were pumping iron or zoning out on the treadmills. With free weight training sections, a strongfur area and some machines, there was something for everyone there, though perhaps not a heaving selection of machines that had garnered complaints in the early days. Variety and variance in training, however, was the spice of life at Amethyst's gym and the mare had had successful month after month since she'd opened the doors of the place. So just who would she be to complain?

A red, chestnut mare with a bright coat, she nipped at the inside of her cheek, tail swishing behind the desk, though it needed a trim now that it was falling near her fetlocks. Other than the white diamond, known as a "star" marking, in the middle of her forehead, she was otherwise fairly nondescript, usually seen in loose jogging bottoms and a vest-top in the gym, paying no one else any mind if they did the same for her. Not many of her gym-goers, however, knew much about her life outside it, which was the way she liked it. In that instance, she was there to provide a service, encouraging, motivating and assisting – but dipping into more personal matters that did not relate to health and fitness, physical and mental, was not something that she particularly wanted to put her hoof in.

She cast her eye out over her little domain, a text document open on the main workstation computer at reception, though her attention was only half on it as the night drew in, darkening the span of space outside the windows. They were mostly blacked out anyway with advertising and branding for the gym, denoting exactly what the warehouse-like building was, set on the edge of an industrial estate, allowing those inside privacy. The gym itself was split up into three rooms, though there was little heating in there: something that would become an issue only in the colder months. But she liked to think that it encouraged her patrons to keep moving and not idle. If there was something particular going on that required greater periods of rest between sets, there was always the ability to turn on spot heaters or heat a single room for those that required it. For her, at least, efficiency was everything.

She leaned on the desk and nodded to a black stallion with a white slash down his face as he left, though he looked a little worse for wear and it wasn't her place to push him for conversation. Soon, she'd have someone else on the desk manning it when her usual staff members had been called out or booked time off, though she still liked to have a presence in the gym. It was all about making sure that everyone had everything that they needed, for her anyway, and that all was running smoothly. She'd been in too many commercial gyms and ones that were in it solely for the money (however one thought that they were going to make bank pushing furs into something they weren't ready for...) to play the same mind games herself.

"Er, hey, Amethyst..."

That caught her attention. Pricking her ears, she leaned forward, the last patron of the evening (for the time being, that was) standing before the desk with what she thought that he might have intended to be a cocky grin on his muzzle. A tall, black bull with almost elegantly curved horns, he towered over her, a good two foot taller, but she did not appear dissuaded at all by that, blinking up at him as he stepped in too close for anyone's comfort.

"Yes?"

Maybe a tad blunt but there did not feel to be anything much more to say than that, waiting on whatever it was that he wanted to spill. She dug around in her memory for his name: Richard, wasn't it?

"Richard..." She tried it, ears flicking to test his response, if it was the right one. "You're here late, aren't you? What's up?"

The bull pulled back shortly but she swore she caught the edge of his nostrils flaring, as quick as it was. In a flash of a moment, everything was normal again, though, still, something wasn't right as he hitched his bag up over his shoulder more securely. It hadn't looked like it was falling off, to her eye. The weight training benches rested in the background before a long double rack of dumbbells, framing his face.

"Ah, Rich is better," he said, regaining some of his usual smirk, the very appearance of it making his smoothly elegant muzzle more recognisable for it. "Just Rich... But I have a problem."

Amethyst resisted the urge to roll her eyes. Was he going to get to the point? Although she couldn't quite put her finger on it (yet), there was something about him that got her back up, holding her words back and her tongue to see what was going to come out of his mouth next.

"Alright... What is it then?"

"Well, you see..." He couldn't keep the smile off his face, that cocky look that she was sure had won over so many ladies before. "I'm coming up a bit short this month and I can't pay my membership."

Ah, there it was. Amethyst's smile grew a little tighter, though she already knew where it was going.

"I'm sorry to hear that. We can pause your membership now, if you like, and then you can come back when things are going better for you?"

Rich, however, was already shaking his head as she talked, not even allowing her to finish a sentence before trying to get his own words in. It was the mare's turn to stiffen, marginally. She hated that.

"No, no, no..." He said, holding up a finger as if to patronise a much younger fur than her. "That's not it, that's not it at all. I'm short on money, but I don't want to *stop coming*, no, that would be silly. I was thinking that...well...we could work out a deal. I could do something for you and then you..."

He trailed off, an eyebrow raised, though it was the bulge rising between his thighs to his crotch that told the tale for him, what he was not willing to actually put into words. Plausible deniability and all that, she was sure, though someone coming on to a femfur, even in the air of trading something like her gym membership for certain "services" was hardly something that could ever be mistaken for anything else, whatever males said of it. Amethyst's eyebrows shot up but, much to his chagrin, her panties did not drop as he had expected them to, the mare straightening her back and pushing her shoulder blades down into their pockets.

"Richard..." She said slowly, working his name over in her mouth, though it still left a foul taste behind. "I'm afraid that's hardly how things work here. Not at all."

Oh, if only he knew how things worked. But the bull was too proud and too cocky, perhaps even a few years younger than her, with a swagger to his stride and hips that told her that he was yet to fall from a manufactured sense of grace. That was alright though: she would happily bring him back down to earth with a bump.

"Aw, come on now, lady," he wheedled, plastering on what may have been a "winning" smile in other circumstances. "You want patrons here, I want to keep coming, I'm sure you need a little something too… You won't be disappointed, I promise you. I can't pay with money but I can pay with, well…this."

He did not grab his crotch but waved his hand before it, chuckling as if it was the biggest joke in the world that she was not leaping into his arms right there and then. Amethyst's eyes flicked to his bag, a designer brand, though not one that she particularly cared about.

That he didn't have the money, she wasn't buying. That he had something else she may be interested in, if not his cock, well…she'd have to see about that.

He still tried like a virgin at a house party, fussing and flaunting, even flexing for her. It would have been comical for her if there had not been a tiny, lingering air of threat there. Any femfur alone with a male would have been foolish to not acknowledge it but that was one of many reasons that she'd taken on self-defence training along with working to ensure that someone would have to really try to hurt her. Her lips quirked in the hint of a smile. Maybe Richard had not seen that she had recently opened up for self-defence classes, for everyone, not just ladies, on a Tuesday evening? After she was through with him, maybe he'd want them for himself…

"I can make it worth your while," he pushed, grabbing her hand, the final straw. "Come on, Am… Am, Am, Am… This is what you want, isn't it? I've seen you looking at me, watching me… This is good for you too, it gives us both what we *need*."

She twitched. *Am*. That hadn't been her nickname for a long time. And she still loathed it. But there were better spoils to be had than simply showing some calf his place in the usual sort of way.

The mare's smirk caught him off guard.

"Oh, you *can*, can you?"

She leaned over the desk, elbows bearing down into it, fingers tracing down from the neckline of his T-shirt. It was fresh, at least, after his workout, though she wouldn't have liked to bear through the reek of the one in his bag. For all the wrong reasons, she squeezed her thighs together, heart racing. The bull, however, wouldn't know what hit him.

"Yes," she breathed, though only someone who knew her would have heard the edge of hardness lacing her tone, cutting through. "And I think there's a little, hm… Shall we call it stress relief? Yes, there's just a little stress relief here that you can give me."

The bull's smirk widened and the mare pushed him back, sending him stumbling on his cloven hooves with his ropey tail thwapping about the backs of his legs. She was on a mission, however, heart pounding, the gym keys in her hand. In a moment, the door was closed and locked and there would be no one else to disturb them for the night, though the cameras were still, of course, rolling. She smirked, hiding her bubbling mirth from him. She might have wanted to look at them later, just to see how much he squealed when she got what she wanted from him.

"Oh…"

The bull grunted and dropped his back, his smirk wavering. Maybe he had not fully expected to get what he was asking for, but he would have to face up to, but he would have to come to terms with it pretty sharpish, a grunt on his lips as he flicked his tail. The bull shifted his weight back and forth, from hoof to hoof, with every breath, though there was no audible feedback due to the thick, commercial-grade matting under his hooves. If it could withstand a barbell being dropped on it with full rubber-coated plates, it could deal with one suddenly antsy and anxious bull.

"Yes…" Amethyst's smile widened, head tilted ever so slightly, walking around him, surveying him. "I don't know why I did not see it earlier, why I didn't think that you would be, oh…suitable. But maybe that is something that's my mistake and, darling, I don't tend to make the same mistake twice. It's a bad habit to get into, you see."

She grinned fiercely, ears pinned, and he tried to match her, puffing out his chest, drawing off his T-shirt over his head. Exposing his bulging muscles at the very least made him look bigger and burlier still, the contrast between them striking. Amethyst had muscle to match but ladies, of course, did not build as much physically as males and her body liked to hold on to the efficiency of it all above all else. That only meant that she was stronger than she looked, her muscles well-defined and noticeably large on her slight frame but hardly bulky and swollen as his were.

Muscles like that weren't going to do him any good, however, while they did her the world of it.

The bull reached for her but, too easily, she slapped his hands away, a scowl on her lips. No, he'd have to fall in line if he was going to grab for her like that, very much so. Richard's lips parted to say something else, but she cut across him, taking charge and taking the lead as things had always been meant to go right from the beginning.

"No. I don't have any need for you to talk. Get down on your knees."

Richard baulked.

"W-what did you say?"

Amethyst's eyes were hard, frozen in her face, though darker than any ice that he had seen, lips pressed together as a muscle jumped in her jaw.

"Did I stutter? Oh, wait, no, that was you. I said, get on your knees. I won't repeat myself a third time, calf, so I suggest you buck up and get on with it."

The bull shuddered and shook his head, stepping back, holding up his hands – yet it was in that moment that he lost his power. He could have blustered and pushed her away or shown her that he was not one to be so easily dominated, yet the flashing uncertainty crossing his muzzle denoted youthful innocence, not having the experience to tell when someone was above him. Of course, the mare should never have been beneath him, that was a silly thought, indeed, to have, but he was too blind to see it, swamped by his own cockiness, however quickly that faded.

He didn't obey, however, and the mare moved in a flash, bending his arm behind him, knocking his hooves out from under him, the sharp, pinching pain of having his already sore arm twisted at such an angle too much for him to bear. The bull squealed and dropped like a stone, neatly to his knees, though that was purely a happy accident, for it was hardly as if he wanted to be there. At least, that was what he told himself as heaved and huffed through his moist muzzle, nostrils fluttering as if they could not get enough breath into his lungs.

Releasing him, Amethyst smirked and stepped back, eyes already casting about for all that she would need.

"That's better. Don't disobey again. Or don't you want to pay off your debts, calf?"

He did... Oh, wait – did he need to? Richard shook his head, mind fogging over, not understanding what was going on despite everything supposedly going to plan. Yet the plan that was playing out at the very moment in time was no longer his at all to command, the mare that his eyes had lingered on for so long collecting a bunch of resistance bands.

"Strip. Lie on the bench."

The short commands were easy to follow but he could not have said quite why he was doing it. Maybe it was part of a game? He was still the stud, yes, still the one in charge, he tried to tell himself, putting a little bit more of a swagger into his stride and step, horns tilting as his cocky smirk returned. That time, however, it was lacking conviction in itself, which suited Amethyst just fine. Calves like him could learn, some quicker than others.

"I thought you'd come around," he drawled, though his words no longer made all that much sense when strung together. "You want me, admit it. You don't have to play games with me, Am, it's really not –
"

"Don't call me that."

He blinked, the tiniest hint of a frown tugging at his lips.

"What?"

Her eyes flashed.

"*Am*. That was never my name."

Huffing, he rolled his eyes.

"Seriously? That's what you're going to pick up on here? Well, if you're going to be pedantic about it, I suppose – mmph!"

He gagged as she shoved something musky and damp with something he didn't want to think about into his mouth, tying it shut around his muzzle.

"Lesson one: don't disrespect me. Lesson two: shut up."

The gag in his muzzle, jaw aching, helped with that second lesson, but that didn't stop his hands from going to it, trying to get it off even when it had only just been put in place. Amethyst clapped her hands, startling him, allowing her enough time to strike his hands with what seemed to be a cane, though it was not like the walking sticks that he had seen elderly furs, sometimes, use. It was shorter than that, one wouldn't have been able to use it for balance or support, and smooth with hardened leather, narrow and *stinging* where it struck. Scowling and mumbling the best he could through the musky, wet gag, he glared at her.

Yet his steps carried him back as she advanced, closing the distance between them, a fire in her eyes that he could not have honestly said that he had seen before. Uncertainty crossed his eyes, but he no longer had the space in which to let his words fly, knees shaking, something in her denoting danger. But where that threat may have been familiar to a femfur if the tables had been turned, the power and the loss of it held a strangely intoxicating edge to the bull.

He grunted through the gag, head swimming, fingers twitching. If she wanted to play games with him and he got his rocks off, who was he to judge?

At least, that was what he told himself, what was easier to tell himself as he wiggled his hips, heat rising to his neck as he slipped down his gym trousers, the loose shorts more than enough for him to get in a workout without them restricting his range of motion in the slightest. It was not unusual at all for him to be naked in front of someone, but there was still an intensity to the mare that he had sought to, well, simply fuck that got the hair on the back of his neck prickling like nothing else ever had.

Yet he was cocky enough to show off his hard-on as it was freed, spitting out the gag after untying it, though the musky aroma of sweat lingered, a heavy taste in the back of his mouth. Maybe it was just a ploy, he thought, something where she thought she was going to get the better of him. Little did the bull know that he was already playing right into her hands.

"This what you want, baby?"

Amethyst rolled her eyes as he rocked his hips, letting his thick length of meat bob and sway. Did ladies usually get turned on by that sort of thing? She doubted blokes did either, but that was not something she was going to waste breath on informing the bull of, turning her back on him as he gyrated.

"Something like that. Get down on the bench."

The cane cracked into the palm of her opposite hand and he started, some part of him jerking to obey. Sure, it was like a bed, he told himself, though that was quite a stretch at the end of the day, something that was a push even if he didn't want to think of it at all like that. The cool of the workout bench, divided so that the seat and the back could be raised or lowered independently of one another, pressed up to his back, and he grinned, stretching his arms over his head. Although his flexibility was not as good as he may have liked it to be after such a strenuous workout, his arms still flexed and stretched and his chest rose, bulging with muscle – muscle that a lot of hard work had been put into. She might as well appreciate all the *bull* she was going to get from him.

But the resistance bands laid across him and he couldn't move his wrists of his own accord as they were tugged down separately and to the side of the bench, bent at the elbows. A quick hook of the bands had his arms straining to their limits, a low bellow escaping his lips, heart racing. Instinctively, he tried to lurch up, but she was already working on his hooves, doubling up layers in her makeshift restraints, locking his cloven hooves down too. The bench itself was too heavy and stable to really be tipped (used in the racks too as well as just for dumbbell work) no matter how much he lurched, bound up in his own soreness too and finding himself unwilling to do anything about it.

Amethyst chuckled throatily, pushing her mane back from her face where the red-brown strands had crept forwards.

"Comfy there? Oh, I'm sure you're not... I'd be disappointed if you were."

Richard grunted and tried to wriggle free, twisting his hands, though the rubbery texture of the bands caught on his short coat of hair, making it easier, even then, to do what she wanted. She made the right thing easy and the hard thing painful – at least, from her perspective. He didn't want to cause himself any strain or pain as much as he wanted to also be free, heaving and rocking, his cock remaining hard throughout.

"Oh, don't worry so much. Most enjoy it."

Richard shook his head, one of the only parts of his body, bar his dangling tail, that he could move still. What was that supposed to mean? And why was his cock still hard? That was, most likely, the only saving grace for the so very confused bull, the ache of arousal coursing through and overruling all else. It didn't matter that he had never before had the tables turned on him in such a way, only that he was there right in that moment, chest tight with something, his loins aching. Arousal and the need to spend a load was more than familiar to a stud like him and he took care of those needs daily (sometimes even more than daily), sometimes with a partner and sometimes alone. The times alone had become more frequent of late, which was perhaps the very thing that had had him thinking with his downstairs brain rather than his upstairs one that day.

Amethyst licked her lips. Yes, it was much easier to adore his body when it was pinned down and restrained, just how she wanted it to be. There was no lusciousness to be had from a stud who thought he could grab her by the shoulders and fuck her senseless, no – leave that fun for the submissive lads, ladies and more to deal with. That wasn't for her and it was never in her to have it pushed upon her, though the bull had crumpled so easily to her dominant fist that she was surprised that she had not seen him already skulking around the fetish play spaces and dungeons of the local area. He really should have given them a go at some point for it was quite likely that there was more there to be had for his pleasure with a dominant hand to control his every want and need.

"It's alright, my sweet whore," she murmured, barely paying the rigid rod of his cock, standing straight up, any attention, the glow of sweat on his body more alluring to her. "This is better for me. And you *do* want this to be better for me, don't you? I thought you had something to offer me, after all."

Still, Richard did not know what to think, panting and grunting lowly, a rumble building in his throat that may have been a nervous moo, though he wasn't going anywhere in a hurry. He was too sore after his workout to break free from the resistance bands and merely arching his back was going to tug at sore muscles. No, it was easier to stay where he was, bound with the bands, eyes wide and chest heaving, though even that movement, sometimes, felt as if it could have been too much for him.

Maybe that was the best place for him to be, after all…

Yet Richard could not help but attempt to rock up to meet her, as tight as the bands were. He didn't know how on earth they were going to come off again as her hand brushed his cock, a fleeting, forlorn touch that was gone as soon as it appeared. It still made his cock throb, however, the flash of lust rising, making him forget the position he was in. Maybe he was right and it would all be worth it to get his rocks off, letting the freak do what she wanted to him for the time being.

Amethyst's clothes slipped off, but she did not care for the show she was giving him, dropping them on the floor in a pile that she would make him clean up and tidy later. That wasn't for her to do and he was soon to get up close and personal with the curve of her ass, the muscles showing through and layering her body into firm, well-rounded definition. Her stomach may not have been as lean as it could have been, the lines of her oblique muscles showing only, but she was in fit and muscular good health, though not one who should ever have been considered a prize of sorts.

The mare smirked. No... She was so much better than that. Furs weren't to be won like prizes but cherished – and that was one lesson that she would leave the submissive bull with, even if he had not realised just how easily he had broken and fallen for her.

It was too easy to stand over him, towering, spreading her legs, watching his eyes widen as her pussy descended towards him. As much as her thighs burned, it was a tease that she was more than willing to push through for the sake of pleasure, grabbing a horn and yanking his head up, forcing him into place.

"*Lick*. Maybe if you're a good fuck-calf for me, I'll give you something in return too."

He grunted into her sex, twisting his muzzle back and forth, but there was nowhere for Richard to go and nothing for him to do but to obey, trapped under her. The sultry swell of her juices trickled forth, laden with sweet tartness, the aroma filling his nostrils as much as he tried not to inhale. There was, of course, always an option for him to resist, to pull back, but the bull pushed on, his tongue out and slithering softly between her plump folds before his mind had caught up with what his body was doing.

"Yes… See, you don't need to be told when you're such a whore for pussy that you're already diving in there like there's nothing better for your tongue to do. And that's right, isn't it? You haven't been taught or trained but you love having your tongue in there, driving nice and good and *deep*… You know this already, but you've never let these thoughts come up, pushing them down time after time again, ignoring them like you have any right to. You're not to ignore them anymore, little whore. Do you hear me?"

She shook his horn, but he could only grunt into her sex, tongue lashing her pussy, wriggling in, though he was clumsy and slopping, leaving as much saliva in the wake of his tongue as he delivered drops of pleasure. That was not anything that the mare was there to worry about though as she ground down and rocked on his muzzle, guiding him, not expecting an answer. He could be dragged into place, if need be, her lusts rising, tail lifting, exposing the velvety dock and the tail hole beneath, though it was only his tongue that would taste that pleasure.

"Unff…"

He groaned deeply and Amethyst's smirk deepened, closing her thighs even more tightly around his head, testing his response.

"You can take it. I believe in you… A big, strong bull-calf like you can take pleasing me. I don't think you thought this was how I was going to be collecting your rent money, now, was it?"

The bull groaned again, sound after sound rolling from his lips as if he was no longer in control of himself and his body. But that was no matter, no matter at all, not when he had someone else to control and take care of him, to dominate him, to tell him exactly what she wanted doing at any given time. Initiative, after all, was something that Amethyst knew only came to the best-trained slaves and pets, ultimately. That was not, of course, something that Richard was going to be instantly able to do and she would be out of bounds to assume such.

Still… He could take direction either way.

"Don't forget the clit… You do need some training. Haven't you ever spent time between the thighs of a lady before? That's going to change. Tease it. Don't leave it. I'm not here for your pleasure, you weak-willed cow."

Richard shuddered. Cow? What? He wasn't a cow, no… No, he wasn't a cow, any kind of cow, and could not stand for her saying such things to him, rocking his hips, though thrusting his cock wasn't going to get him anywhere anymore. His tongue wriggled out of her cunny, however, finding the nub of her clit having pushed out of its small hood of flesh more easily than he could have if it had been his thick, clumsy fingers seeking it out.

He swirled his tongue around and around, tuning into her more and more, the feel of her moans and how they trembled down through her body. He wanted something in that too even though Richard could not, at that time, put words to the desire coursing through him. It was powerful though, a driving need that pounded forth like the beat of his heart, a tune that had to be followed. The bull could no more stop licking her clit and pleasing the mare in that moment than he could stop breathing, for both were essential needs.

Yet the mare ground down with ever-increasing vigour, huffing and puffing, her ears splayed out to the sides as a smile touched her lips. Yes, he would do well, very well, slipping into submission so easily that it was a surprise, even to her, that he had not been doing it for many years already. It was as if everything simply came naturally to the bull, a huff and a grunt from her all he needed to know to go a little harder, to push on a little more, lust and passion taking precedence.

She couldn't hold back and, really, just why would she when there was so much pleasure there for her to take? Amethyst groaned, rocking back, thighs burning but not caring one bit about that. Let her body ache later. It was all part of training and breaking in a new toy and the bull was shaping up to be her most willing slut yet.

"Mmph, yes, calf, deeper again, really get it in there…"

He could only try to obey, not being as skilled in the art of giving pleasure as he may otherwise have professed in other days, the mare's wet pussy bearing down around his lips. Still, he pushed up against her, matching her urgency, the hard throb of his cock driving him on. It was too easy to lose himself in such passions that he had never before spent enough time on, the taste of mare slinking deep into his muzzle, forced to gulp and swallow her essence even as it poured forth. He wanted it all, wanted the most of it, yet it was all there for him to take even if he was no longer a stud and could not claim her for himself.

Richard shuddered. Yes, maybe he understood that in some primal form even then, instinct ruling, throbbing up thick and fast, but it was not to be taken in any other way as his hips rocked and thrust, making the bench judder. It wasn't going anywhere in a hurry, however, and neither was he as he moaned into her pussy, lost in the moment. It was where he was meant to be, something he had never before considered, primarily because he simply had never needed to.

Yet the moment was there for him to languish in as the mare moaned above him, grinding down, forcing him to feel every last tiny moment of her orgasm as her thighs squashed his head lightly. The world around him narrowed to that of her cunny as she forced him down, a hand on his horn keeping him in place, all the bull being good for derided in lapping her pussy over and over again. Amethyst's groans and cries resounded, orgasm rolling on and on, cunny clenching and twitching around nothing, though there was no cock in her to massage and neither would she have wanted one. It wasn't the time for that, even though there were other lusts and passions, even then, to indulge.

No... She smirked even in the height of her climax, thinking of more, wanting more, hips rocking and grinding. There was more still for her newest entertainment to do for her and he would simmer down, turning into the willing sub that some part of her had known all along that he could be. Her tail flicked and lifted, wafting her scent and very light musk over his head, leaving no place for the bull to escape to, eyes closed and his muzzle soaked in her juices.

Richard was hardly present in any kind of reality that he recognised as her leg swung off him, the all-illuminating overhead lights of the gym glaring. They did not allow anything to be left hidden or unsaid in their harsh glow and the mare left him there for a moment, chest rising and falling sharply, cock throbbing more vehemently, if anything.

The bull groaned. Why hadn't he softened yet? There shouldn't have been anything in what he'd done to get him so randy and worked up and yet he felt quite as if he could have cum at any moment, on a hair-trigger of orgasm and working up to it all over again. He grunted and panted, rocking his hips lightly back and forth, yet there was no freedom for him, the tightness of his restraints sending a strange little shiver through him that he could not have said to understand. Maybe later he would but that moment was one for feeling and very much for not thinking.

"Now… I think this will show you your place and nicely collect on my debt, calf. You do know how to take a dick, don't you?"

Her smile teased but the strap-on in the harness tightened around her hips did not. It promised and it would deliver too on those promises, the black silicone rising smoothly out from her crotch. It should have come to no surprise to the bull that it was shaped like a rudimentary equine phallus, although it lacked the medial ring, gleaming as if with a "wet look" effect, the black of it standing out nicely against her chestnut coat.

For a moment, Richard could not breathe, could hardly see, his vision greying out. It was only her hands, gentle but firm at the same time, taking care of his bondage that brought him back to reality. She worked quickly and efficiently, wasting no time, though she did take care to lay the dildo across his stomach while she worked, showing him that it was larger than his, though her position, unfortunately, meant that she could not release him without moving it away. Such a shame, really, but it still added to his humiliation every time that fake cock bobbed into view, reminding him right there and then that his shaft simply could not match up to it.

Yet his shaft did not soften as she sat him up, rubbing his wrists and ankles, although any discomfort there from the rubber bands was faint. He'd never look at resistance bands in the same way ever again but whether that was for better or for worse was something that would remain to be seen in time. For the first time, however, he felt that he had time, not rushing or pushing, merely taking things as they came.

It was not under his control anymore, after all, and he was strangely at peace with that. It felt better to have her hands on his coat and skin in that way, appraising him like he was a bull at market (though that was, perhaps, a little too far to go) and not as a stud. It had been a push to act like that, something that he had fallen into, and she'd stripped him down to the bare bones and true essence of himself already in such a short space of time. Only later would he realise how remarkable that in itself was.

"Very nice… You have a very fuckable ass, do you know that? A lot of those that train do, if they work the glutes, but you have a particularly nice round to them…"

Licking her lips salaciously, she slapped his backside, making the flesh jiggle, and he yelped, though did not move away. Richard did not understand his mental headspace at that time, floating and drifting even though his hooves were, quite clearly, planted firmly on the ground. It didn't make any sense to him, but it was not something that had to make sense as lust and passion washed over him, making him want her all the more, yet not in the same way as things had been when he'd started out. No, things were different, pushing through, his cock throbbing into the brush of her hand as she grasped him and smirked.

"A nice cock… But this isn't going to see any use today. Who needs a prick like this when you have a shaft like mine?"

That much was true, her strap-on pushing out, a good three inches bigger than his and surely thicker around. It was the right way for things to be, he thought dimly, blushing without turning away, his skin prickling with a sense of tingling excitement that he had never before felt. It was new and different and gave him the strange impression that his flesh was on fire without causing him any pain, hips rocking and pumping, need rising. It was there even if it was a different kind of need to what he was used to, breath hot in his nostrils, his nose damp still with her juices. And he wouldn't have had it any other way.

Amethyst snapped her fingers, done with playing. The other end of the strap-on was curved to push into her pussy, giving her something to grind on, while a vibrator buzzed to life against her clit. Some motivation other than his moans, after all, was sometimes pleasurable. An added edge, if one willed.

"Down. Over the bench."

Richard swallowed hard, his Adam's apple bobbing. He could have refused. He could have run. He could have even fought back. He could have paid his damn bill.

"I…"

Her eyes hardened.

"That was an order."

He trembled and shook like a leaf breaking free of the tree in the grasp of an autumn storm, but his knees were buckling before he could stop them. Down and down to the bench, he leaned over it, not thinking of anything else, a gasp and a groan in the back of his throat despite the worry coursing through him. It set his skin prickling in a light sweat, cooling too quickly on his hide, yet he still allowed her to position him there, bracing with his hands on the ground of the other side. A quick adjustment to the height, bringing it up a little more to get his hips at a better level for her, was all that was needed in that regard, the flat of the bench pressing up into his stomach, however padded it was.

"Now… Who wanted to fuck who again? I thought you were a big, brave, stud bull who was going to take me and show me a good time, hm?"

She mocked him, watching just how he quailed from her, yet there was not even a single touch of physical restraint holding him in place. He could have left and yet he chose not to, need winning out as he groaned and thrust his hips, rocking and pushing, grinding into nothing at all. If she was fortunate in his training, she would not even need to touch his cock to have him moaning and thrusting in climax, though that was merely a happy accident to her pleasure, showing him a different way to sex and just why he shouldn't proposition strange mares in the gym with sex. She grinned. It was a lesson that a younger bull should have learned for himself but better late than never she supposed…

The tip of the strap-on touched his exposed tail hole, her hand pushing his ropey tail up and out of the way, but she was not so unkind as to thrust into him without a drop of lube for his first time there. Richard had not had to tell her that not even a finger had made it up under his tail ever before and yet his submission was absolute, breath catching, need rising. He was unprepared but she had a touch of a trick up her figurative sleeve, a small bottle of lubricant tucked into a convenient holster on the side of the harness. Amethyst grinned. That was one that she'd put there herself, sewing it tight and ensuring that it would not come free: quite a handy design.

Pouring the lube down the length of the cock, she applied it generously, letting some pool in her hand as she ensured that every inch was coated with a smooth, pumping motion of her hand. His tail hole beckoned in a twitching pucker, however, that could not be denied the brush of her fingers, two digits easily teasing in. He could not tense forever and the bracing of his position meant that it would have taken him more effort to clench his glutes and tighten up back there than it was worth to him, his body focused on balance and other things rather than stopping her.

Yet the bull could only moan deliriously as her fingers drove deep, sliding back and forth, introducing him to pleasures even if something else that he would find at another time would be that he didn't really need that much preparation. It was only something, right then and there, to ease him into it, squeezing them in down past the first knuckle and all the way to the second, though the positioning was not such that she could add a third. Something in the bull's stomach twisted and lurched, pleasure aching through him, cock throbbing, but the joys of prostate massage could be explored fully through a series of broken, failed, orgasms when she was ready to show him that side too.

That was something for another time, her fingers slipping out and the dildo replacing them, pressing up to his aching hole as the fallen stud bull faltered and grunted. He wanted it but he didn't and it was with that delicious conundrum in mind that he took the shaft up under his tail, her weight easing it in, inch after delectable inch. There was only one way for it to go and that was deeper, his legs braced, hooves digging into the gym matting as if for purchase. Yet the bull did not feel steady or stable there at all, letting out a long, low bellow as he was penetrated, the mare above him letting the gaping hole of his anal ring take all that it could.

Although it was a sizeable cock, his ring was surprisingly yielding and she grunted thickly as she rocked her hips, thrusting and grinding, testing all that he had to offer her. It should have come as no surprise that he was yielding and soft, hardly showing any resistance to her breaking him down into a sub, to begin with, though it was always a pleasure to find. Her hands rested on his hips, gripping him tightly with her hoof-like fingertips, tail lashing the air as the vibrator went to work on her clit. It would get her off even if she did not lean into the harsher and rougher thrusts but it was too tempting to, her pace picking up even as the bull huffed and grunted under her.

"Ohhh… Oh, fuck…"

"That's it, calf," she hissed through her teeth, the arch of her neck dampening lightly with sweat. "Take it all, this is what you wanted. You're never going to get your cock in me, oh no, but I've got a bigger dick than you any day. This is where you belong, under a good lady, taking it all like the little cock slut you are."

Richard groaned, head swimming, tongue pushing out to lick his lips, though there did not seem to be enough moisture left in his mouth to do so. He was just there, a bull along for the ride, broken down into nothing more than a calf without his horns, whimpering and grunting. His anal ring spread easily around the toy with how much lube had been used, a wet slick of flesh parting heralding each thrust, though it was all as he wanted it to be, even though it was not something that he had even realised that he'd wanted before. Maybe it was something that he'd had to experience to know, wrists aching as he braced on the matting, the bench firm under him, a stable force that he could cling on to even though his reality was shifting and turning.

He was there for everything, every last moment of it, nostrils flared as he huffed and grunted, taking it deep. Of course, he didn't feel (and willingly so) as if he had any say in that matter, heaving and rocking back the best he could, though all that the bull pretty much managed to do was roll his hips in place, shuddering and flicking his tail. It tapped up against the mare's smoothly muscled stomach as he tried to contain his lust, his cock throbbing and drooling, although it did soften a touch under the bearing of the anal penetration.

But it felt *good*, so very good that he could not hope to control his grunts and bellows, shifting his weight, trembling in place. He had to stay in place, like she'd said, the slap of her hips on his upturned buttocks rising as she went balls-deep (technically) into his backside. She rolled her hips as she fucked him, reaching places inside him that even he could not have imagined, breath catching, a moan shared between lips. It was strange to be penetrated in such a way, but it was all as it was meant to be, slipping down and down and down into such sweet submission that the mere notion of control was beyond him, whimpering and grunting softly.

"That's it, slut," Amethyst groaned, forcing the words out as her hips worked, tail flagging up proudly at her conquest. "Take it all… You know you like it. You just didn't know that this was what you needed before today."

How could he have? Such was masculinity that so many did not understand how it felt to take a cock or engage or explore in anything other than the more generally accepted norm. But his flesh quivering and shuddering back at her, torn between thrusting instinctively and grinding back for that dose of seductive pleasure, told a tale that his words could not. The bull grunted and heaved, shoulders rounding, though he would have to hold on a little longer as her orgasm swelled in the back of her mind, tempting at ecstasy.

His…however…well…a sub like him didn't always have to get off. She smirked, leaning over him, her hand pressing into the small of his back, dominating so simply and easily. Where there could have been resistance, she only found a willingness to please, simpering and moaning, whispers slipping from his lips like a currency that, one day, he might perhaps learn to trade in.

Not yet though. Not quite yet.

"Call me your mistress, little calf," she crooned breathlessly, a hand twisted into his roughed-up hair as she forced his head back. "That's what I am to you now. And I'll show you how to treat a lady right, not demanding falsehoods in return of what you think is a prize. You're no prize. But you will be, one day, under my training."

He nodded breathlessly, tongue working thickly in his mouth as he tried with all his might to get the words out that he so very desperately needed to spend. It was thick, however, and stuck to the roof of his mouth, forcing him to work his jaw and gasp even then in a vain attempt to force out what he too wanted to hear.

"Y-yes…" Richard grunted, ears flapping, tail lifting, exposing even more of himself to her. "Mistress… I'll do…unff…anything… Promise…"

More words were not able to come as her pace sped up, the raunchy slap of her hips on his backside growing by the second. Huffing through flared nostrils, Amethyst slammed into him as if she was punishing him, yet she had guessed correctly and his bellows increased, bracing for her, his cock throbbing and drooling a stream of pre-cum. Whereas if there was any seed mixed in with that as she inadvertently milked his prostate was by the by for her as he would be cleaning it up, though perhaps not with his tongue the very first time. That could be a step too far but any willing slut, just like the bull, was willing to learn.

"Never try to exchange sex for money again," she hissed through her teeth, ears pinned, imprinting the lesson with each savage thrust of her hips, the vibrator fuelling her passion. "That's not how you treat ladies. Do you…*fucking*…understand?"

Whimpering – though his words were lost in a groan – Richard nodded fervently, Yes, oh, yes, oh, yes, definitely, *yes*, he understood! He had played his cards wrong and that was his due for trying to think he was the top, for it was most certainly not something that he could feel he was when he was pinned under her weight. A deeply seated need throbbed and coursed within in, driven there with the thrust of her cock, yet he could not lean into it, as much as he wanted that lure of strange orgasm, hips rocking, grinding, Richard's thoughts only on the pleasure of the mare behind him.

She was more than willing to think of herself and only herself, however, standing up tall, the flex in her hocks and knees more than enough to put her on just the right level to breed him. His buttocks rolled back at her with every thrust and she moaned out loud, losing control in the best of ways, the need to climax too strong for her. Yet it was not a need that she had to resist, taking her pleasure with greedy gulps, snatching up air as it rolled forth, her pussy clenching and twitching around the other end of the toy slipped up into her pussy, bearing down on it even as she rammed in to the fullest extent that the dildo allowed.

The bull groaned long and low as she used his body for her pleasure, grinding and humping, gyrating her hips, yet the thrusts were not to come anymore. No, that in itself was an act of masculine pleasure and there were better ways still for a mare-mistress to get what she needed, mane hanging over her neck and clinging where a damp rise of sweat had formed in her red coat. She swore under her breath and, still, he stayed right where he was, braced and ready, body aching but trembling with pleasure, all the same, the throbbing of his cock beyond his notice. It didn't seem important to him, not anymore, even though his orgasm and the simple act of getting off had been all that he'd thought about in sex before.

Things had changed. For the bull, they would never be the same again as his tail hole strained wide around that shaft, glistening with lube.

Did he want them to be? Well, only time would tell on that count…

Her orgasm rolled on and on and yet her favourite part would always be drawing out, watching how his hole tried to close instantly and was not quite able to. Left in a slight gape for a moment, she hungrily dipped her fingers into it for the sole purpose of showing him how stretched he was, though the bull was hardly broken.

"I think you'll need a bigger toy next time," she murmured, licking her lips. "Maybe that will give you a little more motivation when it comes to eating out a mare, hm?"

It was a tease and a taunt at the same time, Richard shuddering, shaking his head. But where the shake of his head said "no," the word that slipped from his lips was the same.

"Yes… Yes, mistress…"

He didn't know what else to say as she got him steadied and standing, instructing him to clean off everything that had been tainted by the joining of his bodies. The bull's cock got in the way a little there, bumping up against the bathroom sink as he meticulously cleaned the strap-on and its harness for her, though it was better to be told what to do. Being told what to do meant that he didn't have to think and, as turned on as he still was. It was better, in that moment, to not think, only to be, moaning softly as his body thrummed with a need that was not, at least that day, destined to be fulfilled.

She said it would keep him wanting. She said it would keep him yearning. Even then, he knew it was true.

Only when his cock was once again soft and drooping lightly did Mistress Amethyst present him with a chastity cage. A little too large for him, but only by a hair, it gave him the impression that it could be broken free from, allowing him a modicum of an erection. Yet that fleshing up of his cock as she forced him to get hard, fingers dancing over his nuts, finding his perineum and teasing around the puckered bud of his ever so slightly still gaping tail hole, made it so only a tiny part of an erection could be obtained. Shuddering, the bull huffed and puffed, turning his head back and forth from shoulder to shoulder. He didn't know whether that was a good thing or not but it was, truly, something well enough open for debate. He'd have plenty of time to think about that later, however, as she sent him packing out the door with a key code to let him into the gym at any time.

"Morning session for you, calf, got to work on that back of yours. If you're going to be training and servicing me, I expect you to allow extra time here. I don't give away memberships for free, you know. Eight sharp, don't be late. Oh…and the cage doesn't come off when you're exercising." Her eyes darkened with wicked delight. "That would be too easy for you."

Smirking, she waved him off, the bull not knowing whether his heart should have been sinking or lifting. Regardless, there was a smile on his lips that could not so easily be wiped off as he tottered to his car, striving to work out how to walk with the chastity cage and a partial hard-on, although that would soon become common to him. The bull would learn and come crawling back to her when he next needed her release, though the key would remain dangling from the chain around her neck until then. You know – just to ensure that nothing bad happened to it, of course.

Richard, however, would think of her late at night, lying in bed, sweating, trying to rub himself through the cage. The image of her pussy had near enough burned itself into his mind, something that could never again be replaced or erased, a moan on his lips as he tried to be quiet. The walls were thin there, after all, and it was hardly as if he wanted others to be tuned in and clued up on his current predicament, not even wearing any underwear to sleep in, exactly as the mare-mistress had ordered.

He would be good for her, he would try, yes… Hazily, he drifted off to sleep, unaware that she was using a different toy and pet at that very moment, the bull not even in her mind at all. He didn't know that he was a passing fancy to her while she had become his whole world, opening doors of exploration and lust unlike any others that he could have ever imagined coming to light ever before.

It was a new time and a chapter of his life where he would be able to explore as he willed, under her commanding hoof. Everyone, at some point, needed a guiding hand, after all, and he had gone for far, far too long without anyone at all to even think of pointing him in the right direction.

No, no… No, that was no way for a calf to go, he thought as he drifted off, eyes closing despite the raging need to cum coursing through him. No, he didn't have to veer off track, his cocky demeanour vanished, wanting to be one his knees, though not with anyone watching, exploring and experimenting. Maybe he'd been on the wrong path all along and had only needed one incident on one fateful day to set him right.

Holding the key in one hand as she speared her cunny full on a stallion's shaft, though he was bound up like her little slut too, spread-eagled in quick and easy bondage across the bed, the mare groaned deeply. Her pussy clenched and rippled around the horse's shaft, though his muffled nickers wouldn't get him anywhere as she tried to milk him of his cum, though that would be a particularly difficult endeavour for him, considering the cock ring that she had locked too-tightly around the base of his shaft. No... His orgasm would stay there, right where it belonged.

She smirked, breathless in the afterglow, a hard rod of stallion-flesh at her disposal, the owner wearing a racing hood so that she could not see his features.

"You'll do..."

As changeable as the weather, one fuck, after all, would not satisfy a dominant mare.

That's why she'd had to go and bring one more into her lusty harem.

Crossdressing the Jock

"Well, well, well... Who'd've thought that you would make such a pretty filly?"

Gabriella smirked, the pretty appaloosa mare's tail flagged, though it was not as if her bound boyfriend was about to get a taste of what lay up under her tail that night. Her white coat gleamed with good health, splashed through with black spots all over her hide, her mane and tail thin but combed to silken perfection, hanging down the arch of her neck and buttocks as if they had been destined to lie there at some earlier, prophesied time. A drop of pink on her muzzle, where there was no pigment in her skin, offered a lighter touch of delicacy to her features, though Gabriella was anything but soft and gentle that night.

Her big, bad, tough, jock of a boyfriend, however... Well, it was about time that Noe got a little freaky and kinky with her. A big draft horse with lots of feather around his fetlocks that needed constant maintenance and care, he grunted thickly and shifted in the chair, though he didn't look much of the bulky stud that he had presented himself as when they'd first met, not anymore. He bragged a rich chestnut coat with a flaxen mane and tail, rougher around the jaw with a fuzz of thicker hair, typically masculine with a strongly defined jaw and Roman nose too. Yet all of that paled in comparison to the lipstick softening the velvety touch of his lips, the eyeshadow offering a different introspection to his eyes, mascara lightly applied in just the right flicks of an expert brush.

Noe grunted and turned away, a blush flaring in his cheeks, though a little powder had been added there too to define his features, to soften the edges of stallion-hood that he had been so proud of before. The draft horse tugged at his bonds, the pink bondage rope not something that he would have chosen for himself, but any words that he had had to spend tied around his tongue, his tail trying to flick but catching against the back of the chair, sitting on the dock.

"Erf…"

He shook his head again, but Gabriella only giggled, dressed oh so very alluringly in a mini-skirt and a top that drew the eye to her breasts, not covering her shoulders while the entirety of her chest was hidden: a tease of what a stud-stallion, which he was not anymore, could have had that night. Noe went to lick his lips, but she lifted her finger in the nick of time, stopping him in his tracks.

"Don't do that, my darling, you'll smudge your lipstick. And you don't want to not be pretty now, do you?"

She left the question hanging in the air, though "pretty" was not a word that should normally have been used to speak about a jock-stallion like Noe. His muscles bulged and yet were covered, in part, by a hot pink dress that came down to his mid-thighs. On a femfur, it may have been longer, but the thickness of his body trapped in its curvy constraints rendered it a different fit, even if an appealing one to a discerning eye.

It was wrong, very wrong, but Noe couldn't stop thinking about how the silken fabric felt caressing his skin and hide, how it moved with him, the slightest shift in his body commanding it. It did not cover his shoulders either, leaving them exposed as a more manly part of his anatomy with how well-rounded they were with muscle, though the flow of his mane tickling down and over them helped soften the edges. His mane had never been so plush and well-conditioned, though he didn't quite know what he thought about Gabriella strapping the white pair of hoof-boots on to him that stretched up over his knees. The pleather creaked every time he tried to pull against the rope around his wrists, lashed to the back of the chair, his fetlocks tied off similarly to the legs.

If he'd really wanted to, he could have stood and gotten away like that but there was one little problem to be contested with too. His cock throbbed out of the fleshy folds of his stallion-sheath, forming an obvious bulge in the front of his dress, his cheeks flaring with heat that prickled tantalisingly up into the insides of his ears.

"Ohhh… Seems you like this a shade more than you wanted to let on, sugar."

Gabriella giggled and winked but she was the one in control, the mare's hooves bare, for she needed nothing to cover up the shiny, black hoof-polish she had had him apply for her earlier that evening. They'd been supposed to be going out but that no longer seemed like much of an option, not when she wanted nothing more than to stay home with her kinky sweetheart. He was much better as a filly-wife anyway, not a jock. Gabriella shivered deliciously, a tickle of lust creeping through her. Why hadn't she gotten him into such things before?

Ah, there was no time to worry about that, not as she kissed Noe's cheek, the stallion grunting, his cock throbbing all the more vehemently.

"What's that, cutie? You have something here for me?"

Giggling, she walked her fingers up the small span of bare thigh visible between the boots and the hem of the dress, tickling the bulge with the dancing tips of her fingers. As was the case with most horses, her fingertips were harder and more hoof-like, as if the entire tips of her fingers were tiny hooves. Sometimes it flummoxed their dexterity just a little but was not something that was usually much of an issue for them.

He trembled under her touch. Why did it make him feel so sensitive, as if he was going to explode from that alone? The dress pushed up more as his cock strained, bulging and growing, blood rushing to all the wrong and all the so very *right* places. To be bound, resisting, struggling… It made him feel small, weak, as if his girlfriend suddenly towered. To a young guy, who was still finding himself in the course of his college studies, funded by his football scholarship, it was a strange and foreign emotion twisting in the pit of his stomach.

Still, neither did he try to resist as she slipped the dress back up and over his shaft, letting the fabric caress the base of his sheath as it tried to spring back down into position. Noe trembled. Even that light touch felt as if it was too much for him to bear, his grey length of cock a little darker as the flesh wrinkled at the base, the medial ring appearing strong and firm. The head was flatter than it was for most other anthros in their world but not flared right then, though it did not feel as if it was far off.

"I think a pretty filly like you should have a reward…"

His head spun. A pretty filly? Was that what he really was to her? Did he even want to be? His breath caught in his throat as he grunted, some manner of desperation pulling inside him. Yet it was not a feeling that he could put words to as his heart pounded, something tightening around his lungs, breath restricted.

"Breathe, sugar, breathe."

How did she know? How could she have possibly known that he was struggling, yet Noe gave over yet another sliver of control, leaning into her control over him all the more gratefully. Everything was easier if he just listened to her. So, all he had to do was listen to Gabriella and everything would be alright – more than alright, in fact.

The mare caressed his head, sliding her fingers around and through his mane, combing it out. He was beautiful like that, though he probably hadn't realised that she'd added a little padding to the hips of the dress to give it shape before dressing him in it. It had started off as a flirty play, something of a joke, but had escalated to him bound and "trapped" in the chair at the dressing table of the bedroom before either of them could catch up with themselves. It was a far push for a relationship that, considering their stage in life, was still in the earlier stages, but something that had come a little too naturally to them.

Gabriella could not have said whether it was good or bad, but it was something she would consider and think about later when she didn't have a delicious hunk of filly-jock right there before her. It was better to focus on the present moment.

"Darling…"

She caressed his length reverently though delicately, as if Noe really was a weaker filly than her, one that she could "break" if she was too rough with "her." The stallion, however, shuddered under her touch, the thick length of his cock throbbing within her fingers, swelling and pulsing, astonishing her all over again with his vibrant virility. He snorted heavily, mane falling into his eyes, but the mascara was more than good enough quality to stick despite a disturbance. She wouldn't have used something low-quality, after all, on her previous filly…

But Noe was only present in the moment of her touch, grunting thickly, trying not to press his lips together. She'd told him not to smudge his lipstick and there was something about the slick, soft caress of it on his lips too that he wanted to savour, even if he could not be quite sure why. Was that how it felt to be a mare, a filly like Gabriella? His girlfriend's body was a lot more delicate than his and yet she was the one that held all the power, his cock bubbling up with a hint of pre-cum, shocking even him.

"See, I told you this was something you'd like," she teased, though she had not truly known whether she would have been able to persuade Noe to try it or not initially. "Relax, cutie... Pretty fillies like you don't need to worry about anything."

Not to worry... Not to worry about anything? Oh, that was a nice thought, very nice indeed. He didn't have to think about needing to be the biggest, the strongest, the best on the pitch. None of that mattered anymore as Noe got his first taste of submission, tail flicking back and forth, though he'd only later realise that it was trying to flag, exposing his holes to his girlfriend. Sometimes the body better understood what the mind wanted than the mind.

It was a tease and a taste, feeling soft and feminine, not even the feel of her pumping his cock in long, smooth strokes enough to make him tingle with masculinity again. Even that word choice was wrong, the notion of "tingling." He should have been throbbing and pumping, thickening... Masculine, strong words. Yet all Noe felt himself to be was a weak little filly in a dress who needed to be taken care of by her strong girlfriend.

It was tempting, so tempting, to lean into Gabriella's touch, the mare's expert fingers folding around as much of his length as she could reach. He was modestly sized for a stallion but still had a cock suited to please any mare, thick and wanton, pre-cum slurping forth in a tantalising bubble. The mare did not wipe it away either but allowed it to trickle down the fat meat of his girth, smearing it along his smooth length, the skin wrinkling lightly and smoothing out again where the lubrication allowed her palm to move more easily over him.

There was nothing else for him but the present moment, his mind wrapped up in the stroke of her intoxicating hand. Even the scent of the perfume that she'd spritzed on his neck, the pulse points there, twirled through his nostrils as he heaved for breath, chest rising and falling sharply, need escalating.

"There you go, filly, this is what you need…"

Control came more naturally to Gabriella than she could have expected, licking her lips, eyes dancing with dominant delight. Her tail flagged proudly, though it was a triumphant raising, knowing that she'd "captured" her little filly to do with just as she'd pleased. She'd never wanted a big, strong jock to fuck her and ream her and leave her dithering and simpering in the aftermath – no, never. It was not her fault that Noe had swept her up and off her hooves though, breaking her sense of who she thought she could fall for in the world.

The mare was only fortunate, very much so, that he seemed to be very much into the same things that she was, opening doors for them to explore further.

The stallion had no restraint to play with, however, arms bulging with muscle as he struggled. He couldn't help it, something deeper pulsing in his loins, nuts aching, the tingling throb there feeling strange and foreign, not quite like the precursors to orgasm that he was used to. Yet Noe could not remember a time when a hand or even a warm cunny had moved so easily and softly over his shaft, caressing him rather than pumping him. As a stallion, it was all about being rough and hard and he'd leaned into that prior without thinking. Though it had only taken Gabriella to show him a different way, another inclination to the fetish and lust that could be shared between like-minded partners.

His thighs tensed, muscles aching, straining, yet there was nowhere for him to " and nothing for him to do as he broke in a whinny that was "girlier" than any he had ever given, cock throbbing with spurts of hot seed. He could not control it, but it was no longer up to him as she coaxed spurts of creamy cum from him, dominating his body in a flirty fashion, as if it was all a game to her. Gabriella cooed as his cock shot its load, aiming it away from his body, telling him that he shouldn't get his dress dirty, though Noe heard it all as if from a great distance away as if she was in the lightness of air and he underwater, hearing it all through the crushing, lustrous weight of it.

But the pleasure, oh… Oh, that could not be denied, coursing through, pump after pump coaxed from him, though his only regret was that the male orgasm was not as long as that of a female. Gabriella could rock and grind her pussy on his lips for what felt like minutes in a particularly strong orgasm, though it wasn't that long, even if longer than his. As the last spurts and dribbles of seed left him, his cock softening a little, he groaned, ears slanting back, panting heavily, his nostrils flaring harshly with every breath he managed to snatch up.

Gabriella whickered, tail flicking back and forth in a luxurious swish of hair.

"See? It's better with a little kink involved. But now… I think you owe a mare a taste too."

She untied the knots holding him there without removing the ropes, allowing him to feel the looseness for himself, even if Noe was not truly free. No, he was caught under her command and spell, grunting softly, his cock soft again as he locked his gaze on to the sensual sway of her hips as she sashayed her way back to the bed. The crimson sheets complemented the black and white of her hide perfectly, a goddess laid out for him, her top slipping off, exposing her brassiere, her heavy breasts barely constrained by it.

With a wiggle of her hips, while he shook off the ropes and stood, teetering, in boots that he was not accustomed to wearing, she squirmed out of her mini skirt too, revealing that she wasn't wearing any underwear. Noe whinnied softly, nostrils quivering. Could she have done anything more to be any hotter for him? He didn't think so, the mare before him perfect exactly the way she was.

She spread her legs for him, revealing her pussy, the pink folds of her sex beckoning him in like a precious flower. Yet it was not one that he would crush, approaching slowly, feeling large and ungainly in both the boots and the dress, something different about the way he moved. He couldn't put his finger on it though as he tried to pump his cock back to full hardness, as difficult as that was when he'd only just got off.

Her eyes landed on his shaft, though Noe had not expected the curious scorn he found in her blue orbs.

"Oh? That?" Gabriella shook her head, licking her lips, but her eyes had already drifted from his shaft. "Oh, I don't need that little toy… Find a big dildo, bigger than *you*. Maybe that'll be enough to please me."

Ears pricked shamefully, Noe released his half-hard shaft, still drooping as if it had never been destined to rise to full mast again. Maybe she was right but the thought of him not having a large enough dick (as was the way of masculine pride in the bedroom) to please her. The toy box offered an option, however, and he selected the largest toy inside, a smooth, purple, silicone shaft that had a rounded tip.

"I don't need lube. I'm horny enough after teasing you, filly."

Noe shivered. She was soaked, he could tell, upper lip trying to curl back to sift through the scents in the air, though he wanted to preserve his make-up still. Gabriella wanted him to look pretty, after all, so it was up to him to be the prettiest, cutest little filly in the world for her.

He teased the toy between her folds, joining her on the bed, the dress pulling tightly around him and restricting his range of motion in ways that he could not have expected. Yet it remained a constant reminder of the position that she'd put him in, the toy sliding through her juicy wetness, her folds glistening with it.

"Suck the toy."

He stiffened.

"What?"

It was one of the few words he'd uttered before donning the dress, nostrils flared, eyes wide. Gabriella only levelled her gaze with Noe's, daring him to deny her.

"You heard me."

He blushed fiercely and yet was surprised to find himself obeying, even if he could not have said it was the most natural thing in the world. The stallion's lips parted curiously around the shaft as if he was tasting something new for the first time, sliding it deep, surprising himself with a grunt as it pushed over his tongue. He sucked it as he imagined she sucked his shaft, his cheeks hollowing faintly, Gabriella watching his every move, her hand between her legs, toying with her clit.

"Yeah… That's it, baby. You're such a good filly for me, such a slutty girl. Take it nice and deep now."

It was almost a point of pride to do as she asked and Noe half-closed his eyes as he pushed the big toy back over his tongue, moving towards the rear of his mouth. Equines had no gag reflex but that did not mean that it was easy for him to gulp around it as the fat head, thickly rounded, pushed into the back of his throat. His throat bulged faintly as he swallowed around it, his girlfriend moaning, fingers working away in her sloppy pussy, slick with her arousal beyond anything that he had ever seen before.

"Yeah… Yeah, filly, just like that."

He sucked on it all to please her even as she worked herself up into a panting, nickering frenzy, eyeing up her boyfriend sucking on that dildo as if he was a professional, slurping on it, swirling his tongue around. He knew her eyes were on him, her moans just for him, though he could not stop, grunting and thrusting the toy into his mouth again and again as if he was a slut-filly on "her" knees taking a huge dick.

Maybe that would be the next thing his girlfriend had him do?

It was too much for his mind to take in that moment, cock throbbing back to full hardness. It was too sensitive to touch but he had more important things to do, playing the part of putting on a show for her, slurping and sucking on the dick in his mouth, ramming into his throat, as if his life depended on it. Nothing else existed, nothing else mattered, only pleasing Gabriella, being her slutty little filly on show, taking a cock that was big enough to make both of them neigh in climax.

Gabriella's hips lifted from the bed, hardly able to contain herself, rampant lust coursing through her with every beat of her heart. As much as she loathed cutting short the show, she dragged him in closer to her by the wrist, eyes burning with a fierce intensity.

"Fuck me with it, filly – hard! Get me off!"

Her demand lashed through the air like the crack of a whip and he obeyed in the blink of an eye, the dripping dildo sliding from his lips, lipstick lightly smeared on the length. That no longer mattered anymore as it smudged and smeared, plunging the toy into her sex, knowing exactly how much she could take as Gabriella clutched at him. Her hooves dug into the bed as she nickered and neighed, vocal in her lust, calling out for more, demanding it – and it was all that he was willing to give.

Submission, sweetly so. That was the gift he had for her right there and then, plundering her pussy with the sex toy until she squealed in a squirting climax, soaking his hand and the toy, dripping on to the bed. It was what he could offer Gabriella as her sweet little slut-filly, her newest and favourite sex toy to play with. He leaned over her, lips tickling her clit, tongue flicking out against it, though there was only so much that Noe could do as her hips bucked and ground, raised for his attention, demanding everything that he was already delivering unto her.

Eventually, however, orgasm spent itself out through her body, the mare collapsing in a lightly sweaty mess, juices trickling down her thighs. There was a very obvious wet spot left on the bed, but it most certainly would not be Gabriella who cleaned it up when she had a filly to take care of such mundane matters for her.

"Mmm… You're such a good filly."

Smiling faintly, she stroked her boyfriend's head, tucking a stray bit of mane out of the way behind his ear, his eyes plaintive, fixed on her, appearing more feminine in that moment than he had before. Her body pulsed in the afterglow, the tiny aftershocks of orgasm tingling a hair's breadth below the surface, her girly boyfriend blushing prettily all over again, leaning into her hand, letting her stroke his mane.

"Th-thank you… Ma'am."

Gabriella grinned.

"Ma'am? I like that… But there's something I like better. When you're all dolled up as my pretty filly, I'll only be your mistress from then on. Never your girlfriend, never Gabriella. Do you understand, filly?"

There was only one answer he could give her, sucking in a breath through parted lips, the caress of air over his lips and tongue still strange, but a sensation he would become more and more used to. After all, she was going to use him as her pretty filly many times over as their relationship developed.

"Yes, mistress. Always for you."

Thus the door was opened to something new, something that would bring them closer together than ever before.

Tempting her jock to cross-dress was the best decision Gabriella had ever made.

His Submission
at Her Hooves

He exhaled softly, his nose tipped down to the ground, the bull submitting as if it was simply something that came naturally to him. Andy should have known better than to go back to her, the dominatrix who adjusted what she offered to each individual client, but he had always thought that he was more than just a client to her.

"You submit too easily."

Andy shivered. As a bull anthro, that was true. Everyone expected him to fight back, to be burly and brash, blocky and bold, but he was none of that. When he was exhausted from putting his black coat and silvery-grey horns "out there" in everyday life, in his high flying but excruciatingly boring office job, it was Mistress Amber that he turned to. The mare was beautiful, so small and so light – and yet that only added to the power she held over him.

In her "treatment room" – what the official tax forms that, once, he had completed in her service while in chastity had said – he was only a slave. His submission was willingly given and Andy would never have denied that he paid for her services, if pressed, though he did not advertise it either. The name that he used with her, if she even took the care to use his name, was a nickname anyway. His mistress, despite everything, did not need to know the name that he formally went by, not for what they were doing.

"Horns all the way down to the ground. You're slacking."

He was and he knew it, rounding his upper back and tipping his head even more to keep the tips of his curved horns on the ground. It was not a comfortable position, but that was not why she asked him to do it. The mare was beautiful, when he was allowed to look at her and otherwise, her coat the glowing gold of a palomino. Her mane and tail cascaded in a flow of white, spun fine like silk, and, sometimes, when she bored of using him in other ways, she had him comb out both her mane and her tail until they gleamed with an even more lustrous glow.

Andy liked that too. The bull wasn't in it, after all, just to get his dick hard. It was the taking away of control, even if it was him, truly, that was giving it up, that he lusted for. He didn't need more power, more control, to have more and more responsibility lumped on him when, always, it would be the bull who took the fall for it. Nobody had ever asked him, outside Mistress Amber's sessions, whether he wanted that much responsibility. But they'd told him to take it all anyway, regardless of what he wanted, what he thought.

With her, it was different, him nude, willingly so, his cock and balls out. On the smooth floor of her play room, he grunted softly, rolled on to his black. He hardly knew how he got there, though sometimes time didn't seem to have any meaning when he was with her. Even if he sweated and even if he ached, there was a sense of peace to being with her.

Mistress Amber crouched, resplendent in a latex corset, the neat tuck of her waist even more alluring than ever with the tight lacing. Her hips flared out with matching, dark-fabric panties that hid enough of her to be mysterious and draw him in, a garter belt hitching up the latex stockings so that they stayed perfectly in place. With her neat, pale-coloured hooves, she didn't need shoes or boots or anything like that, not in her natural state.

Her eyes though… They pierced right through him. Even as she stroked his cock, testing his readiness, his hard prick throbbing into her hand as if it was meant to be there.

"There now… Isn't it better to be like this?"

He grunted, but didn't need to say anything out loud. Andy wasn't all that sure that he could speak out loud, not anymore. He didn't want to think, only wanted to be, as she used his body, fitting heavy, metal cuffs around his ankles and wrists. They were more restrictive than latex, leather or anything else. At least, they were to him.

"Up."

The metal weighed him down but the bull's studly length of cock led the way. He licked his lips, stifling a cry, her hand suddenly grasping his shaft. He may have been taller than her, but he could not have felt any smaller and more insignificant than he did at that moment, panting, nostrils flaring damply.

"Such a whore-bull, aren't you?"

She forced him to address it, words leaping sharply from her lips as if the lips from where they came. It didn't seem right, didn't seem natural, not with her natural beauty at play, the golden hue of her coat…and yet, still, it was inexplicably so. Some things, after all, were merely as much a part of Mistress Amber as they were lacking in those that, daily, she took care of.

"You don't need a dick like this."

He shuddered.

"No… To be blessed with a dick you can't even use… How pathetic is that?"

He whimpered, swaying lightly from one side to the other, though she only drew his hands over his head, a chain running through the O-rings on the manacles. The bull trembled as the chain rattled, sinking through his being, cutting through right to his soul. How could that be so?

His arms were pulled over his head, words raining down, his legs forced apart, though she fixed the spreader bar between his thighs rather than his ankles. That was new. Confusing, but new, offering a different restriction in motion while his arms were kept aloft, chain winched high so that he had to stretch up, just a little, to stay in place where he was supposed to be. His muscles strained and bulged, though Andy did not do all that much to stay in physical shape, only weightlifting two to three times a week for maintenance only. He didn't even want to push that part of his body beyond what was required.

No… He still had to work out what he was, who he was. But that was okay when Mistress Amber was there to show him.

The mare did not have to be a predator to appear predatory, stalking around him in a tight circle, licking her lips. The bull knew he was perfect, at least to her, merely for the fact of what his body could do for her. His hard cock throbbed, the tip marked with pre-cum, but she did not pay that part of him any attention at all as the round meat of his glutes drew her eye, a little softer than Andy may have liked his body to be.

"You… You need training."

It was a bland, flat statement and yet Mistress Amber still managed to strike a chilling thrill into his body, his spine tingling in a strange way. He didn't have to do anything, for all was in her control.

Yes… He thought. *Yes, train me. Breed me, break me, beat me, use me.*

It was hard to say those words out loud, which was perhaps one of the things that she already knew about him. Mistress Amber always seemed able to tease such things out of him, even then.

"First training session. Orgasm control. You do know a little about controlling yourself, don't you, slut?"

Andy shuddered.

"Yes, mistress."

Not really, but he wanted to please her, wanted to do something, anything, all to please her. That was all he craved, grunting thickly in the back of his throat, the mare donning long, latex gloves that went up past her elbows. They were so long, in fact, that they almost impeded on her ability to move, though his eyes widened sharply when the bottle of lube came out.

Lube… Gloves…

Oh no.

He didn't have to think and yet he still snorted moistly, shifting his weight back and forth, the oddly placed spreader bar suddenly feeling an awful lot more restrictive than it had been. It was tight, too tight, and gave him a farce and a pretence of balance when, truly, there was none that he could so easily take for himself. Andy bellowed softly, fear coursing through, though it was a kind of anxiety that made him want to thrust and grind, a willing participant as much as Mistress Amber pushed his boundaries.

She was glorious and he could cling to that if he needed something to root him in the moment, to remind him that training was not so bad. As the lube drooled over her latex-clad fingers, it rendered them shinier and more slippery than ever, though he could not turn his head too much, for his horns came up against the chains that kept his arms over his head. It was a tiny note of restriction, but it almost forced him into obedience, considering that he didn't want Mistress Amber to see him looking. Not unless she wanted it, of course, but that was only something that he could hear from her own lips.

"Steady, slut."

To be her slut, willing and abused… He held on to that thought. It was what he wanted, what he yearned for, letting go of his daily reality. There was no one better in the world to do that with other than

Mistress Amber. Forever would she be everything to him.

But she did not need to know that and she swept all thoughts of that from his head as her fingers probed at his tail hole, the entrance to another release and reality for him. He moaned out loud, for there was no way for him to hold back, her finger sliding into him.

Mistress Amber did not have to tell him to relax, for he knew that drill already. It was gentle but would not be for too long. He grunted, trying to contain it, knowing there was more to come – and another slick digit filled his backside a moment later. He wriggled, squirming back and forth, panting hotly, striving with every part of his body to bear through it, gulping and moaning, eyes watering.

The best or the worst of it had not even come as yet. But that was how it was, how it was meant to be, leaving him tottering and teetering on the edge of something more, something that pulsed through him devoutly, threatening to tip him overboard. He grunted, tipping his chin down, his nose moist with breath, though Andy was not there to at all be in control of himself, not at all. It was the way of it to hump and groan and rattle his chains as a second digit teased into him, her fingers expertly curled up against his prostate.

"Do not cum."

It was a given, but it still made him gasp to hear those words said out loud. They slipped over him like silk and, still, he could not drink up the water of it, moaning softly, helpless to her whims. If he was to be a good bull for Mistress Amber, he would have to submit to her training. Yet that submission had to be found sometimes, the route there not one that he had to walk before.

His cock ached and throbbed, drooling a clearer string of pre-cum as his prostate was teased and milked, the pressure making him buck and thrust, working his hips lightly. It had to come, had to be played with, but she had told him not to, sending his head spinning into confusing, completely coming against his emotions in a sharp juxtaposition. Andy moaned and tried to rock back, though his position there was so precarious that he could barely move at all, straining his abs, contracting all that he could to stay in place, though it was to no avail.

He was going to fall at her knees either way. It was only a question of when that would come to pass.

Three fingers inside his tail hole. He tensed when he needed to relax, panting and heaving, his chest shuddering. Sweat gleamed on his head, as if he was nothing more than a piece of meat, strung up to be enjoyed. Maybe he was, to her, lust rising, shifting his weight, muscles tensing and relaxing as if that would release some modicum of tension, making the greater span of it easier to bear.

It didn't work like that, however, not as he rocked his hips lightly, pushing back against her, his cock throbbing, drooling. The clearer stream of pre-cum her milking touch forced from him was not to be unexpected and yet the need of it all swamped him, forcing him down, locking him deep in submission from which there could be no rising from, not even for him. He had no qualm about what was happening to his backside, as much as his ass already strained around her, another dollop of lube pushing her hand deeper.

"I'll be disappointed if you let go, bull."

He shuddered. No. No, he had to do what she wanted, always holding on to that, the need to please her. His backside ached, her fourth finger folding in, all pressed together as if her fingers were making a cone.

He felt every last millimetre of them sliding into his backside as she stretched him out more and more, working her fingers back and forth, her digits pressed up to his prostate.

Andy hissed through his teeth, struggling, straining, locked in place when all he wanted to do was to thrust manically back and forth. But that would have thrown him off-balance, shoulders yanked back and dangling from her chains, and he would have been nothing more than a disappointment to the mistress that he wanted to please above all else. Nothing else existed for him other than her as he whimpered and grunted, striving to swallow his lust, cock aching, the tip tingling as if some manner of fresh sensitivity had been drawn on without him even realising.

"Good pet… That's better. That's a start."

It took only one moment to push her training up a notch as she folded her thumb in too, Mistress Amber not satisfied, not yet, with his performance for her by far. She would take him, have him, control him, make him see why it was better to give up that control that real life forced on to him, so many times over. The mare snorted softly as if disparaging his efforts, his mind attributing meaning to something that was merely in his head.

But that was the way that brains worked, pulling meaning to things where it did or did not belong, each huffing, wet breath overwhelming him. For her fist slid deeper and deeper, his first stage of training, grinding in deeper, forcing his backside to stretch beyond what, in that moment, he thought was possible.

He had to release, had to cum, though none of it seemed at all as he had felt it before, so many sensations confusing with one another, coming up in a mess of feeling that could not be untangled in the heat of a moment like that. The chains rattled as the bull strained and pulled, gasping, panting, lost in the moment, her fist disappearing inside him, even though the lube helped. It did not soften the bulge of her fist in his ass, however, stretching him out for the first time in that way, for she had never gone that far with him, teasing and testing that boundary. Though Andy supposed that that teasing and testing made sense in hindsight, even as his head spun and spun with lust.

"That's it..."

Her breath caressed his shoulder warmly and yet he could not hold back, all ramping up sharply, fingers pushing up against his prostate, once again giving the weak bull no choice in the matter. More and more slick pre-cum trailed in a strange string of lust from the tip of his cock, milking him with her fingers, forcing a tight burst of pleasure through him, though the cord in his loins was so tight that he could not do anything about it, panting, heaving, his whole body wracked.

His shoulders ached, arms pulled back out of position, pain layered through, but his cock was harder than ever, impaled on her fist, everything lusciously coming together in a moment that he most certainly could not have played out on his own. It wasn't for him to control, of course not, the mare pumping her fist inside him gently, his ass sucking around her wrist, though someone on the outside might have wondered just how his backside could take so much.

Yet anything was possible with the right attitude and a mistress to tease his body through it, bucking, humping, grinding, chains pulling. It didn't make sense, the strange, strained pleasure that was not true ecstasy, pre-cum milked from him... Or was it something else? He'd never had that before, feeling on the brink of orgasm and not at the same time, left there, hanging, dangling, though that was not a threat that he longed to hold on to. For, if it broke, it would plunge him into true ecstasy while she fisted him, panting, moaning, grunting, stomping weakly with the spreader bar still locked in place.

He didn't know how long it went on for, but it was not true orgasm, not as confusion pounded through him more avidly than any cock. It was impossible to tell, yet she played his body to the beat of another drum, an instrument that he had no hand in at all, tense and pushing, grunting, chewing and licking. There was no way for him to release.

Only under her control her fist working back and forth, fingers toying, playing, stilling as his cock leaked and leaked. His broken and wantonly abused body strained with desire, sweat marking his hide, though there was a part of him, as his lips moved soundlessly, that could only crave it more and more.

Whatever she was giving to him… Oh, he would have it all over again, if only to serve her, to serve her so very passionately. The mare chuckled throatily without a hint of amusement, tail flicking, though he only knew that in the sting of the long, luxurious hairs lashing his thigh. The pain had his cock softening, easing down as if he had really ejaculated, though the bull could not even be sure, right then and there, what had happened.

Maybe that was what the true loss of control was all about? He snorted, head tipping, swaying. He could not know, could not say. Only Mistress Amber could. And she was all that mattered.

Panting heavily, the failed orgasm – for it had left him needier than ever – washed through him, the bull hung his head. He could not even remember his own name in the aftermath of it all, ropey tail swinging back and forth, thwapping weakly, not even strong enough to swat away imaginary flies. Before her, his mistress of the moment, he was nothing, he was weak, he was malleable and something that, even then, could be shaped and turned to her whim.

He was nothing without her, he thought dimly, his backside strained around her fist, even as she slid it back, slowly, so very slowly. His cock could have throbbed to full hardness again, yet his body did not feel that it had the energy for even that, continuing to soften and naturally shrink to its usual state, drooling and dribbling odd pre-cum (to him) the whole while.

"Better, pet... Relax now."

It was not soothing, but it was most certainly an order as he hung there, his shoulders strained into an awkward position, though she could not help that, not with him. It was for the bull to obey, mindless and nameless, panting open-mouthed, sucking in all the breath he could as her hand, finally, eased from his backside.

"Ooohhh..."

He groaned, closing his eyes, though the gape of his anal ring was not to be left there to tighten up. He could imagine how it was, even then, the dark hole of it begging attention, perhaps even slick with a gleam of lubrication, heralding his pleasant debasement, how he had been milked, how he had been used. Had he even truly been able to obey her order not to cum? Did that count? It was not for a bull submissive, like him, to judge. Not to say, only to be, only to do what she ordered.

That was the least of it all.

He flinched from the push of something thick against his backside, though it was not bigger than her hand, even if his eyes opened again. It had to come, had to ease into him, pushing deep, a thick butt plug finding a home under his tail. He could have submitted quietly, but there was still a part of him that reacted and responded, intelligent and sharp to the last moment, pulling on every last scrap of energy to flick his tail up for her.

"You are learning."

Was that a note of approval in her tone? He hoped so. For that was all that he wanted to hear, over and over again, until his heart ached with the weight of her approval. He groaned softly, her fingers pushing at his tail hole, seating the butt plug in fully, though it had not been given any lubrication that time around, his anal ring stretched enough and backside well-lubed to allow it inside.

He was good, if only he tried, if only he leaned into everything he was, all he could be to a mistress, her or someone like her. The bull snorted, wriggling his hips, imagining that he could get that butt plug even deeper inside him, all to please her. Of course, like many other designed, it had a large, flared base after a narrow neck to ensure that it stayed right where it was supposed to be, his chest shuddering with snatches of breath.

Her fingers played over his backside, digging into muscle, need rising. But it was not for him to say what would come of the rest of his session with Mistress Amber, her fingers stroking his nuts, easing around, weighing them in her hands.

"You don't need these to be accessible."

It was a statement, not anything that was to be argued with, as she rummaged for something, leaving him there. She could take her time, for every second where she was away from him dragged out the tension more and more. His skin itched, cock throbbing all over again, though it was there for him to swallow down, licking his lips as his shaft threatened to swell ever so slightly.

But Mistress Amber was there to see to that, something metallic and restrictive sliding over his shaft, though he could not have denied that it was a tight fit. A ring went around the neck of his nuts, keeping it in place, and he craned his head down with wide eyes, the mare's deft hands securing the metal chastity device around his genitalia.

He grunted softly, but did not complain, even as his dick swelled, throbbing up against the bars of the metal cage, which encased his cock so tightly that it was not possible to break free, even if he had wanted to. It gave the impression that his flesh could bulge between the bars, though he whimpered, the tightness inescapable, a lump rising in his throat.

"Wear this until you next see me. Do you understand?"

The bull could not manage to get out the words that he wanted to say but he could nod, eyes closed, hanging there. A part of him had thought that his time with Mistress Amber was over, but the equine loomed despite being shorter than him, fondling his shaft, tapping her hoof-like fingertips over the metal with a short, sharp clack of sensation reverberating through him.

He grunted, head spinning. He'd never felt anything like that before. Her lips brushed his cheek, though he did not react, frozen in place as his tail flagged, lust rising, throbbing up thick and fast to the forefront of his mind.

"Now, I have a chore for you to do."

Groaning, he swallowed hard, though that still didn't ease the lump in his throat. More? What more could she possibly have in mind? One thing was certain, however, was that his session was not over yet.

He yearned to throw himself into submission at her hooves again and again. Nothing would keep him away, no matter what she put him through, what she nudged him to try, guiding his path into release repeatedly.

It was not over yet. And the bull would forever remain Mistress Amber's loyal pet. His cock throbbed.

Imprisonment in chastity was only the beginning of it.

Female Dominance

"How does that feel…pet?"

I shivered. Oh, she knew how it felt, my big, dominant, dragon mistress, a good head and shoulders taller than I was. I was just a gryphon, smaller than her, weaker than her. My feathers were pretty in shades of silver fading to grey and white speckling through my furred half, but I could not match up to her splendour. I was just a trophy for my mistress, the dominant being who had claimed me and taken control of my leash. And that was just the way I liked it.

I didn't want a thought of my own, not as I hung there in suspension bondage, my wings even outstretched in a faux expression of flight. I could not fly, of course not, not with such little wings, as pretty as they were. My arms were bound to my chest, hands up near my collarbone, horizontally placed as if I could have just beat my wings at any moment and sprung up into flight. I didn't need my hands for that, of course, wings held out through an intricate line of pole bondage, where they were delicately and firmly bound without damaging a single feather. It would have been easier for her to put my wings in a sleeve behind my back, but maybe she just liked it.

I didn't know. I didn't ask questions. I was just a good birdie boy for my mistress as she prodded the ball gag in my beak. My ebony beauty – well, she was not mine… A pet like me could not own a mistress… That was not the way it worked. I loved her, but her black, glowing scales were not for me, oiled and adored solely for her pleasure.

That was one of my tasks for Mistress Vanity even though she was far, far from vain. I had to care for her, to groom her all over, applying special oils to her scales to keep them in the best of condition, that was after I'd bathed her. But she was ready for more, to use me to satisfy her lusts, while I was just her little amenable toy, something that could be picked up and put down as and when she pleased. I wasn't good for anything else, but to be her pet and her toy was all that I yearned for.

Grunting, I chewed at the ball gag, though I did not have teeth within my beak to do so. Mistress Vanity laughed and pushed me away, my legs straight out behind me, though I knew the bondage and ropes would keep me levitated and safe. I'd never once fallen from suspension bondage before and I had no reason to believe that, even once, my mistress would ever let me down.

"Pet… I'm bored."

I shivered. Oh, that was never good. But there was nothing I could do for her, no answer I could give her, not as the full-figured dragoness stalked around me like the queen she was. She knew that she was in control and her power came from, well, her, control locked within her hands. Mistress Ebony groped my hide, squeezing my ass, claws digging in, but with the gag in my beak I was denied even the ability to squawk.

Just the way she wanted it, stepping out of my line of sight. Typically, a pair of blinkers had been attached to the bondage on either side of my face, further limiting my vision. My breath raked against my eardrums as if it was being funnelled in the wrong direction, swinging back and forth, grunting, heaving, though every sound I made was light and faint. She didn't want me to be too loud, after all: that was why she had gagged me.

"Little whore… You could squeal for me, but where would the fun be in that? I'm going to fuck you, again and again, until you are sore and aching and loving every goddamn second of it."

That was something and more than enough for me, more than my mistress usually wanted to give me.

That must have meant that she had something very special in store for me.

For her pleasure, of course. Not mine. When I was nothing more than her submissive servant and pet, my feelings and opinions did not matter. That was one of many reasons that I loved her so much.

"Mmmmph!"

Her fingers slid under my tail, ignoring the leonine length as it twisted back and forth. A quick, cursory lubing up of my anal ring was all that she wanted, for there was to be no pleasure taken in it from me. I grunted, wriggling my hips, the ropes moving, shifting, my body swinging. There was nowhere for me to go and, frankly, none of it mattered. Not even as my cock pushed out, swelling from my small sheath, though it was more of a slit when it came to what was tucked up at a gryphon's crotch. I'd seen others that were so much bigger than me and I just didn't think that I matched up to them, not even with my little nuts hanging behind, mostly hidden in the grey and white fluff between my legs.

Mistress Vanity didn't say a damn thing as she stepped up behind me, pressing the tip of something hard and cold up to my tail hole. I could have tried to fight it, even if I wanted it, but that would have been pointless when I wanted it so much. I wanted to be used, even as she shoved the dildo savagely into me, clearly wearing some kind of strap-on.

She didn't need to tell me, not one little bit. There was nothing, nothing at all, that my mistress would ever need to do as she ground into me, thrusting and pumping, grabbing at my suspension bondage, the ropes, all to get more leverage to push deeper and deeper.

It was, by far, the largest toy that I had ever been told to take, however, my backside yawning wider and wider, the smooth, round head of the toy penetrating me deeply. Behind the ball gag, I grunted and squalled, yet my mistress was not about to let up, not when her favourite, best of toys was right there for the taking.

"All of it... You're going to ache for weeks and weeks after this..."

I knew that was not true, but it still sent a wonderful shiver through my body, aching deeply, moaning and whimpering. Mistress Vanity did not hear me, not as she moaned and licked her lips with a lewd, wet smack, thrusting, pumping, driving in, again and again, using each thrust to push a little more into me. The cock seemed to get wider as it moved towards the base, though there were, thankfully, no raised bumps or ridges to make it even harder for my poor, abused ass to take.

It burned, though my cock stayed hard, strangely so. I usually got a little softer when I was being penetrated, but something in me tingled deep down as if it was burning up from the very pit of my being, deep down within my stomach. My dick ached, even though it was so small, so insignificant, not the kind of cock that could please my mistress. I shuddered, trying to yawn my beak open, though even that method of releasing a small amount of tension was denied to me. What was wrong with me?

Nothing, of course. It was only my mind grappling with pleasure, the blurred line where strain became pain. I didn't mind a flicker of it, as long as it was all in service to my mistress, as my life had been devoted. That was why I took every one of her strong, driving thrusts as my stomach leapt and quaked, moaning behind the gag, even though my cries would not be heard.

As long as I was a good hole for her to fuck with her strap-on cock, I was a good pet. As long as I was pretty and presentable in my bondage, I was a good pet. Mistress made things easy for me, but that never, not even once, stopped me from trying to be my very best for her.

Forever and always.

My ass strained and my cock drooled, what felt like a thin stream of pre-cum trickling to the ground. Any mess I made there would have to be later cleaned up with my tongue, though that was all well and good, all that was needed, grunting, groaning, a slave to my emotions. Even then, I wanted to fall prey to it, to grunt and to buck and to thrust, wild and untamed – but that was just why I needed my mistress to tame me, to dominate me, to control me.

She thrust and thrust, powering into me, the dildo feeling as if it was reaching up deep inside. It had to be long, very long, but the details of it all did not matter as I grunted and groaned, drooling around the gag as if I couldn't manage to keep my own saliva in my mouth either. My mistress was kind to me, I thought dimly, though even my thoughts felt as if they were moving dully and thickly through a layer of sludge. She took care of me, used me... That was all a pet like me was for.

My body was hers, completely and utterly, all to do with as she willed. I whimpered and groaned, but my cries fell on deaf ears, if she could even hear me. My body ached deeply, cock throbbing, a faux orgasm forced from me with each milking thrust. The toy ground over my prostate and yet that was not something I could take true pleasure in, my body growing steadily more frustrated. It *felt* like an orgasm but not at the same time, cock leaking, drooling, my need growing with every passing second.

I couldn't hold it back and yet there was nothing to hold back, my body trapped and aching as if I was constantly on the edge of orgasm, my mistress pounding me, her breathing coming more and more heavily. There must have been something in or on the strap-on to give her that extra touch of pleasure too as she thrust, heaving over me, my whole body swinging from the ropes.

"Yes… Mmmph… Such a good slut you are!"

She hissed those words out through her teeth and yet my body would still have been there for her to do with as she willed either way. She didn't have to make my heart sing with humiliation, but she did it anyway, even as she threw her head back passionately, howling out her lust. The scent of her orgasm licked at the air and I only wished, in that moment, that I could have shoved my beak between her thighs and eaten her out, over and over again, all to give my dear, sweet mistress every drop of ecstasy that she deserved. But that was not what she wanted that night, not as she fucked me more savagely than ever, my ass aching, though I was surprised that my body had accepted it.

My head drifted, fading in and out lightly, as if I was present in the moment and not really, both at the same time. Such was the delight of sub-space, of feeling as if I was so deep in submission that I never again had to come back up to the surface. I would have stayed down there forever if I'd had the choice, but I had to remember that that, along with the massive cock shoved under my tail, my mistress controlled that part of my life too.

She brushed her fingers over my lower back, checking in with me. Weakly, I chirped behind the gag, flicking my tail back against her chest. I could feel her smirk in the air.

"I'm hardly done with you yet, pet…"

I knew that. I always knew that.

That was why I submitted to her female dominance, the power of a mistress.

It was the only way for me.

Training a Slave

Finley groaned, lowering his head, the Doberman's nose tipping submissively down to the ground, though the carpet was more than thick enough to cushion his knees, even though the canine anthro was nude from head to toe. His striking black and rich orange-brown fur was on show, his muzzle a little narrower, a little more elegant, than what one might have expected. His tail was not docked and curled up lightly from the root of it, though the glow of colour on his muzzle was what drew the eye, the orange-brown marking coming up closer to his left eye than his right.

"What a good little pup you are..." His owner crooned, though Mistress Elle was his wife too, even if they weren't considering that part of their relationship at that time. "Are you going to behave for me? Are you going to be a good boy? I don't keep bad boy slaves, you know..."

She looked down imperiously over him as her tail flicked back and forth, the elegant white fox with a smile on her lips, though it did not reach her eyes or bring any manner of softness to her muzzle either. Her tail was thick and full, fluffy where Finley had brushed it out for her, caring for her from head to toe. Of course, a mistress did not need to be nude unless she wanted to be and she wore long, thigh-high boots with a shine to them, the black perfectly contrasting the purity of her white fur. There was a shocking heel on them too, but, well, Mistress Elle wasn't going to be walking around for much, not with a slave whimpering before her, so very eager to please her.

Finley shuddered, his eyes travelling up her body, kissing her boots softly. The dog knew that he was allowed to do that, worshipping her boots and, by proxy, the hind paws that were clad inside them too. He would spend hours upon hours on her paws too if she let him, not because strictly he had a fetish for them or anything like that, but massaging them and ensuring that his mistress didn't have to carry the stress of the day along with her in her paws was something he *could* do for her. For a slave, it was something inside his control, something he could do for her. As much as he wanted to give up his control to his mistress, he wanted agency to please her too. It was not about being bound up into a drone-like toy, not for them.

Well, that could be hot too, but not that time, not that night. Her thighs were exposed, arctic blue underwear covering her pussy, though Finley more than knew what lay beneath. A corset cut across the bottom of her ribcage in blue and black, matching the rest of her attire, though her breasts were covered. A twinge of disappointment pulled in the pit of his stomach. He wished he had the liberty and grace to adore her breasts that night too. But that would have to come another time.

That night, he was only there to serve his mistress, to be trained in her whims and pleasure, however she pleased.

She'd been sitting in one of the dining chairs, in their shared living room – no, that was not right. He whimpered and pressed his forehead down to the ground, his backside shoved up in the air as if he was trying, even then, to expose his tail hole to her, to show her every last bit of how wilfully submissive he was. He didn't want to hold back anything from her, not from his mistress. His tail didn't need to flip up any higher than it already was, but he still submissively laid his cheek against her boot, rubbing it back and forth.

"I am a good boy, mistress…" He breathed, though it almost didn't feel right to even speak in her presence. "Please… Train your slave. I want to know everything I can do to please you, always."

Mistress Elle looked down at him imperiously, grunting deep in the back of her throat, though it was almost a sound of discontent.

"Oh, will you?" She said, turning up her nose at him as if he had done something to displease her. "Then, pup, you're going to have to prove yourself, aren't you?"

The living room was quiet around them, their house detached and the windows, of course, securely closed. There was no trouble there for them, no worry about them being overheard, more than free to play out their bedroom fantasy in every way that they knew how. Only, the dominant and submissive part of their relationship came into even more than that too, perhaps in how he could best serve Mistress Elle from the time she walked in the door at the end of a long, hard day.

"I will prove myself, mistress, I promise. How may I serve you?"

The vixen made the first go easy for him, for which Finley was grateful. He didn't want to have to guess too much, even though he would have been more than glad to adore every part of her, from head to toe, if that had been what the fox had wanted. He could do everything for her, willing to try most things, if not everything – or, at least, that was what his lust-addled mind thought in the heat of the moment. That was, at least partly, why he needed someone in control of him, someone who could temper his desires, to show him what was safe and sane, though it would always be consensual for him and her.

He moaned, slipping between her spread legs as she sat back comfortably on the sofa, though the vixen was not trying to watch TV, not when there was greater lust at play. Mistress Elle smirked down at him, though there was only love behind her gaze, for there was no one in existence who could honestly claim that, in domination and submission, love could not be present. There was no softness there, that was true, but Finley didn't need there to be.

He only needed to please, following her direction as he shoved his nose straight between her legs and lapped over her pussy through the fabric of her underwear. It was silk, high quality, and he knew he could not be like a feral creature and merely rip it from her body, no. No, it had to be treated with as much care as he always treated his mistress, always holding the fox in the highest of regards. There was nothing else that he longed for other than to please, thinking of her and her alone as he grunted, teasing her pussy in long, smooth, slow strokes of her tongue.

There was more still that he needed, but her pleasure was all he could think of. She groaned and whimpered so very softly, so very breathily, rocking her hips up to him. It was only a light roll and a push, though that was all she allowed him, training her pet, her loving pup, all so that he could please her even more sweetly.

He took his cue, taking over in the giving of pleasure as he tugged her underwear gently to the side, allowing his tongue to stroke over her folds directly, sweeping them lightly apart as it sensually dipped between them. Oh, he could have spent days savouring the honey of her on his lips, an addiction of the highest order. Why, Finley could even have gone without orgasm if it meant that he pleased his mistress, getting everything he needed from serving.

"Mmm, that's a start, pup…"

She stretched out her legs a little further for him and he could almost imagine her toes curling within her boots, missing some of the little cues from her body. Yet her pussy was so sweet that he couldn't help himself, lapping deeper and deeper, though he resolved to only get her off, that first time, using his tongue and muzzle. He wanted to show her his skills, proving himself to her as her slave and pup, always close, always lusted for, always useful to her.

That was the best thing for a slave to be in his fantasy, which he longed for, moaning for, whimpering for. His tongue delved inside her, seeking her G-spot, over and over again, flicking over it, though he knew exactly where her pleasure lay. The first time didn't have to be slow, not when there was so much more to come, and he swapped between her pussy and her clit, delving into her with long, desperate laps of his tongue and swirling back up and around the sensitive nub of flesh.

The vixen revealed signs of her need, arching up against him, though the pup didn't mind that. He wanted her to feel good, even if it meant that he had to move his head a little more quickly with her, riding out her orgasm, lust curling through the two of them in the best of ways. Yet he was the submissive one, never destined to be on top. Even if he had ever been allowed to take a top position, it just wouldn't have felt right to him and, even when he had tried that in the past with other partners, it hadn't been fun to him.

That was why he wanted to be a slave, not exactly mindless but still wanting to learn how to be better, to do better for her, always. Her clit throbbed lightly within his lips, squeezing around them, lapping and suckling, and he focused all his attention on that, pleasuring her, doing everything that he possibly could for her. Nothing else had to exist for the canine, not when he was pleasing her, listening to her little breathy pants, the moans that rose.

Her need was there to be fulfilled, after all, and he held tightly to her with his muzzle between her legs as he moaned, letting her hump and buck against him to her heart's content. Mistress Elle did not tell her pup when she was close to orgasm, for it was not needed, nothing was needed. All she had to do was to feel, to experience that pleasure, lust rising, her orgasm dripping down his chin as he lapped and lapped, sensing how much pressure she needed from his tongue.

The vixen was at her most beautiful, he was sure, in the throes of climax, though he could do more for her than that, yes, he was sure, so much more, licking off his lips and resting a willing paw on her thigh. The ripples of climax still ploughed through her in the afterglow and he rested there, waiting, already thinking about what he could do next for her.

"Mmm, that was a start, pup."

He bobbed his muzzle, keeping his eyes downcast.

"Perhaps my mistress would like a massage?" He offered, trying to take the initiative, to show that he wasn't just going to be a passive partner even if he was playing the part of her slave. "I could rub your back, I bought some special oils for you, mistress, they're good for your fur and your skin. Or I could make you climax again, rim your tail hole, I could put on a display for you, a show..."

He blushed. That would be a hard one indeed for him to do, though he knew that his mistress enjoyed watching him. And he wanted to make sure that she was entertained, that she always had eyes on him in a good way. Wasn't one way to show her that he was going to be a good slave, the best of them, by doing things that she loved but weren't entirely comfortable for him? He would do it all for her and it was not as if his pleasure would fall by the wayside there.

"Hm..." He knew that look on her face, how Mistress Elle pretended to contemplate things. "A massage is a start, pet. Bring me my favourite drink first."

Finley did that swiftly, hustling along. A gin and tonic: but the gin and the tonic had to be exactly right, with a kind of ice that had to be frozen in a special tray and cooler within the freezer (Finley didn't quite understand it all himself) so that it came out like cut glass, so clear. It made a difference, to her, and he was more than happy to go through everything she wanted, using a twist of fresh lime also to colour and add a touch more citrus to the drink.

His mistress was lying down on the sofa when he returned, her corset loosened at the back so he could reach, though Finley already knew where the vixen held most of her tension. The lower back was a sore spot for her, from spending most of her days at a desk job, and he was extremely keen to lavish attention on it, letting her take a sip of her drink through a conveniently placed straw. He'd thought of that so that she didn't have to get up again to have a drink, allowing her to enjoy the moment more easily.

There were no instructions given to him as he massaged her, showing his worth, softly accepting his role. It felt right to linger there, to relax into it, to not worry about anything other than the acts of service. No more mattered and it would not matter at all, not even after that point, not as he let a submissive mindset completely and utterly envelop him.

It was safer there, warmer, softer, bolder, allowing him to be simply as he was. He groaned, rubbing her back, sliding his paws down over his backside, though his mistress acted like he was not there. She sipped her drink and even flipped through a magazine, though the fox could not hide the twitches of her ears back towards him, showing that she was, indeed, paying attention to him, and how her tail lifted a little more when his fingers kneaded into a particularly sensitive spot.

Her glutes were tight and he spent time working on those, her underwear back in place. They were sodden between the thighs, holding her aroma, and he grunted, holding back his desire. And yet it was not so easy for a dog like Finley to tuck away his arousal, his sheath plumping out as his pink shaft slid into view. He had already been pretty turned on anyway, but feeling her backside and smelling her erotic scent was too much for him, swelling through.

The pull of her… Oh, she was intoxicating, the best kind of addiction. And Finley knew that to be true even as she rolled over on to her back, pushing him off the sofa, revealing that she had been hiding something under her.

"Put the straps tight on me, pup."

It was a simple thing, a strap-on harness that was already fitted with a long, thick dildo with a slight curve to it, three ridges near the tip, just behind the head. The head was thick, tapered to an off-centre point, one that he had had inside him many times before. If he knew his mistress as well as he thought he did, there was most likely a hidden tube of lubricant in the sofa cushions.

His tail lifted, wagging – even though he was worried about taking a shaft like that with little preparation. Sometimes, things just had to come through like that and he would at least have the lube. He was just a dog that liked to be prepared and brought up slowly, though that didn't mean that the pleasure, for him, would be any less like that.

No… It was just a different kind of pleasure, the kind that his mistress dictated. She would never hurt him, not unless it was deliberate, with whips and clamps and all kinds of kinky things…

He groaned. Helping her into it was natural to him, sliding it around her hips and her legs, the straps easing into place. They were leather, so very soft and pliable, that they all fit comfortably. He knew that too, for the vixen had had him wear it too sometimes, just so he could fuck her without his cock sinking into her, stopping the dog actually feeling any pleasure at all.

The strap-on had a bullet vibe on the inside, though rather a large one. It helped spread the vibrations through her crotch and folds too, stimulating her clit directly – especially when she ground against it, cock buried deep in his ass.

"Back to me, pup."

He did as she asked, putting his back to Mistress Elle, though the vixen did not ask permission to yank up his tail and slid a lubed-up finger around his tail hole. The dog shuddered. Oh, she worked quickly! He shouldn't have expected any less from her, of course, considering that they had been together for a good few years already, though he still loved how much she could surprise him. He loved too how she controlled him, how he always knew that his mistress had his best interests at heart.

It was good to know that he was being looked after, relaxing as a finger and then a second slid into his tail hole, stretching out the Doberman. His tail still wagged, cock out and bobbing, though Finley would have been a fool to think that he would get off that night.

Getting off was not for a slave. Even for one that was being the best boy, the "goodest" of pups, to his mistress.

He knew that. But that didn't mean that the want for orgasm was not something she could use to control him.

As if in a dream, the dog was drawn back on to the fake cock, the hard length of slick silicone pushing deep into his asshole, slowly stretching him out, more and more. He whimpered, letting his head fall back, her paw on his hip guiding him down. It would not become a mistress, even in such a position, to thrust.

No… Oh no. It was for him to grind down on her, to think about how riding the strap-on cock was giving her increased pleasure, the vibrator sending light vibrations up through the shaft into his backside too. He pressed down and rotated his hips, shifting back and forth, humping and grinding with the long, fat cock shoved into him to its fullest extent.

"Ohhh…"

"What cute sounds you make, slave," she murmured. "Maybe you were built to ride my cock, like this… Just like this…"

Her moans rose, unashamedly enjoying herself, the pulse of pleasure through her rebounding into the submissive dog. But the vixen had only her interests in mind, even though she was there to look after her pet too, to make sure that he had all that he needed then. For what he needed was not only orgasm, which could be held back, but the denial of it too, held there, beautifully on the edge while he grunted and moaned, trying to hump back against her crotch with raw desperation.

Her chuckle was music to Finley's ears and he growled lightly, even though he was comfortable where he was, seeking out her orgasm. He would have it, yes, would please her, would make her feel good, would think about her, only her, no matter how hard his cock was.

His length ached and dripped pre-cum on to her thighs and he blushed heavily, leaning forward on to her, trying to get an even better angle to grind back on to his mistress. It didn't quite push the dildo up against his prostate in a way that he would have wanted, but it felt better to him to please her and, well, he could hold back from orgasm a little better that way. His mistress, after all that, wouldn't allow him to cum and had most certainly not told him that he could cum, so far.

Finley, thus, could only assume that he was not permitted to cum, his lips twitching, trying not to growl too loudly, grunting, groaning, need coursing through him. His mistress said something that they didn't catch and he whimpered, head rolling back, her paw crawling up his body to clasp his throat.

It was so tight, so dominating, all in a way that had him quivering under her hold, moaning, wanting more. He had to have it, had to give it, his mind confused, bouncing back and forth, moaning aloud. All Finley wanted was to make her feel good, pressing down all the way, his guts lurching, need pumping through him, heartbeat after heartbeat. There was nothing like the feel of that thick, slick cock inside him, imagining that it belonged to his mistress, that every clench and shift of his tail hole around it even gave his mistress pleasure.

"Mm, that's right, slave," she yipped, eyes alight, pleasure getting the better of her. "Take it... Make me come!"

It was an order and a demand and he didn't want to disappoint. No, no, no... That wouldn't have done, not one bit, not to disappoint her when all he could have ever focus on was her and her pleasure. Mistress Elle deserved so much more and he pushed through the mild discomfort in his tail hole – nothing, of course, that would actually hurt him – to grind down. He had to take the vibrations into him too, even though he didn't want to get close at all to orgasm, even though his cock was hard.

The drooling drips… He bit his lip. He'd have to clean those up later, most likely with his tongue. But he didn't mind that, of course not, even if it was his own pre-cum. It would all be in service to his mistress, after all, and that was better than anything.

"Harder, slave!"

The demand came with a snap in Mistress Elle's tone and he moaned as he leaned into it hungrily, wanting more. Her paw was still on his throat, reminding him of his place, and he shuddered to consider just how easily she could draw him into her grasp. It was intoxicating, all in the best of ways, making him quiver and whimper, lusting for her, wanting her, desiring her more than anything else. There was no one else in the world that he thought he could ever lust for and love as much as her, though Finley would never get the chance to find anyone else. He simply wouldn't want to.

He grunted, pressing hard into her paw, losing himself in the moment. There, he didn't have to think about anything else other than how good it felt to please her, to serve her, to be dominated by her. There was no bondage present on his body and yet he was chained to her more strongly than anything else, feeling the links in the manacles, everything that weighed him down and in place.

Willingly. Always hers, always her willing, obedient slave, so much all for her.

He felt his cock hardening and willed his orgasm to stay away, even though it felt like there was way too much surface tension in his body, crawling deeper, pressing up inside him as it did every time. Sensations had to be played into account too as he panted heavily, losing some of his ability to breathe as her paw closed in tightly on either side of his throat, bearing down on his windpipe.

Finley liked that even more, though it was the control of his mistress that got him off, when permitted to go all the way. He leaned into it, whining, lifting his tail, giving her the best view possible of her faux cock sinking into his tail hole, again and again. He put on a show, grinding and rotating his hips, the need in him stringent, powerful in a way that could not and would not be set aside. He could only imagine how stretched his anal ring looked from behind, the lube slick and shining on the shaft of it.

"Yes, slave… Keep going…"

Her tone was not soft there, but hard and biting, as if she wanted him to know the power she held over him. Her eyes bored into the back of his head and he arched out his back, pressing his chest forward, wanting to be good for her, his black fur glistening and shining with sweat. Still, he pressed on, grinding down, humping, whimpering, moaning, forgetting his own lust instead of hers, the only one that mattered there. So far down in sub-space, without even realising that he'd blissfully fallen, the dog twisted back and forth, trying to get even more of the toy inside him right at the point of Mistress Elle's climax.

She howled, her lust overcoming all else, filling the room as if her arousal and orgasm was a tangible force that could surpass even the air in it. It made his insides ache when he bore down that hard, but he knew what he wanted, rolling his hips back, all to make the vibe tease against her clit in just the right way.

It was exactly what she wanted and she rewarded him for that when she came down from her high, softening, easing, panting for much-needed breath. What was lost, in her case, had to be regained too, though he rose from her, knowing what she wanted.

His neck ached deliciously from the pressure of her paw, though he wanted it even more, panting, whimpering, taking care of her. The toy slid from his tail hole and he fully took on the role of a slave and servant, taking the strap-on back off her and setting it aside to be cleaned. He sorted the gentler needs in the aftermath efficiently, using a warm, damp cloth and wiping it over his mistress' thighs while she stretched out. There was still some of her drink to be enjoyed and she sipped at it, lying lazily half-curled up on her side, tail resting over her hip and thigh as if it was a blanket of sorts. Even though it was thick and fuzzy, it was nowhere near enough to cover her.

"Take my underwear off, slave. And the corset, fully now."

The boots stayed on, but he removed all else, caressing her fur tenderly.

She sat up, leaning back on the sofa, patting the space next to her.

"Come here, pup. Lie down. I want your dick in easy reach."

He didn't know what that meant, what pleasure she sought from him next, but Finley had to try to understand, one way or another. He did as she asked, though it was hard to do it without touching her, so much so that Mistress Elle clicked her tongue impatiently against the roof of her mouth.

"Faster!"

She hitched his legs up over her lap, dragging him into place so that he lay with his legs over her lap, cock in easy reach. The dog lay on his back, ears submissively splayed. Even sitting there, above him, the vixen looked so tall, so imposing, so lustful. He loved every bit of her, from head to toe. Even more so when her paw closed around his achingly hard cock, sweeping and stroking up and down tantalisingly.

"Mmm, so hard, so needy…" She said, though it was as if her attention was not truly on him, as if she was distracted. "I didn't think slaves could get this aroused. Maybe there's a use for your cock, after all."

Oh, how he hoped so. That would be wonderful, amazing. Finley whimpered, trying to be as appeasing and as appealing to her as he possibly could be, tail wagging back and forth under his buttocks. It was half trapped there, though it didn't really matter, only that he was doing what his mistress wanted.

And she was being so kind to him! The dog didn't think that she had been going to touch his cock that night, but maybe she had had a change of heart? Having his best interests at heart did not mean that she had his orgasm at all in mind, even after all that. He groaned, relishing in the feel of her paw going up and down, pulling the skin of his shaft lightly back and forth, feeling as if he was going to blow right there and then.

So close to the edge, he moaned, pre-cum drooling down his cock, marking her paw, though that could have been the deciding factor for the vixen. For she looked down at him with an imperious look of disgust, wiping off his pre-cum on his fur and brushing his shaft, when he had been so close to orgasm, with the tips of her fingers.

He panted, eyes wide and shining, need coursing through. Of course, that didn't mean that there was any respite for him, his mistress already moving on.

Fuck, I love her…

And it was all part of his training, all in holding back his orgasm, in being denied. Finley would only understand that later.

"Maybe next time, pup," she murmured, letting her hand drift from his cock as if it was a forgotten fancy to her. "Maybe next time... Fetch me another drink. I have more in mind for a slut like you."

He grunted and nodded, cock bobbing in the air before him as he sought to do her bidding. Sure, he was riled up and horny, but that didn't matter. It didn't matter at all, only made him even hornier and harder for her, lusting for her. Some would have said that such a high level of arousal even made him keener for her pleasure than ever before.

Maybe that was true, maybe it wasn't. But seeing his cum explode from his cock by no means was important.

He mixed her drink. He served her on his knees. He spent a good portion of the rest of the night between her legs, pleasing her to orgasm after orgasm.

Not once did he cum. A slave didn't deserve that. And Finley loved every second of it.

Not as much as he loved his mistress though.

A Dragoness' Feet

They were so soft, so warm, her scales small and neat down there. And I spent rather a lot of time down there under Mistress Onyx's feet, the jet-black dragoness radiating power. It was the best place for me, her personal foot slave, though the title was one that I entered into willingly. Even if I didn't live with my dragon mistress, her weak, ever-loving scaled slave, I yearned to spend even more time with her than I already did, the dragoness dominating my thoughts even at work.

In her bedroom, she sat on the bed, perusing her phone, as if there was something there even more interesting than me, under her feet. I kissed her sole reverently as she moved her foot over my face, where I laid on my back beside the bed, in the perfect place for her to toy with my face – and the rest of my body too – with her feet. As always, everything was exactly as she pleased, just as it was meant to be.

However, my body was not important against hers, though my scales were softer and more skin-like, as if to show vulnerability. Mistress Onyx was beautiful, a stunning, statuesque beauty who towered over me. I was only just about touching five foot five, which was a little on the short side for drakes in my country, but Mistress Onyx did not care about that. She loomed ominously, dominantly, over everyone, being seven feet tall – but that only meant that there was so much more of her to adore and serve, day by day, even hour by hour. Her horns were a faint silver, a line of silvery spines running down her back, though the membranes of her wings, the leathery folds between the spines of the dragoness' wings, were only silver when light streamed through them, translucent and captured by the light.

"You're slacking, foot slave."

I shuddered. Oh, I loved when she called me that, when she wriggled her feet on my face like that, how clean and fresh they were, though they did not yet smell of anything other than her naturally, light aroma. They were the most captivating part of her, of course, her toes delicate even though they were larger than my own, everything about her larger, stronger, her tail curling back and forth as I whimpered and took a toe between my lips, carefully. I knew what Mistress Onyx wanted and I was more than eager to give it to her, swirling my tongue around the claw on her toe, suckling and pulling her toe deeper into my mouth.

Heavens... If only I could stay down there forever, not have to work and become Mistress Onyx's full-time slave, never having to wonder or want for anything more. I would even do all the housework, care for my mistress full-time, if only it meant that I could end the day being her foot slut, kissing and lapping over her toes, massaging her soles, fingers running down to the heel of her foot so very tenderly.

The dragoness sighed and my heart pounded. Was she getting distracted? Was I not doing a good enough job down there? Shoot, I had to do more, always more, my mind locked on to serving and pleasing her: all as it should be. I could not disappoint her, my heart going out to her, whimpering, kissing the underside of her tones, my tongue flicking out, wriggling between them.

Nothing existed for me other than her feet, my world narrowing to them. My cock was hard, my arousal high, my body naked... And yet I couldn't concern myself with anything like that. My pleasure was not her concern, not when I was there to serve, carefully ensuring that her foot was perfectly clean, wanting to move to the other – but I had not yet been presented with it. I could not be demanding of it, no, not to my mistress, serving her needs and lovingly setting my own aside.

It was not the place of a foot slave, after all, to consider their own needs. That was never what I wanted to do.

"Use your hands, foot slut."

I whimpered. Oh, I even loved the sound of her voice, how low it was, seductive, like velvet, as if I could lose myself in it. I didn't need to be careful of my claws, for they had been filed short, out of the way for her. She leaned back, ignoring me, her back flat on the bed while I used both hands to massage her feet, which were larger than my head. My fingers expertly, even while I laid there under her on my back, worked down the arch of her foot, down to the underside, around the heel. Oh, there was a lot of tension there and I could not set that aside, murmuring my sweet appreciation of her, knowing that I had to be there for her, I had to adore her. There was nothing else, not in the whole world, that I could possibly do.

I kissed her toes reverently, praising her with soft murmurs and whispers. There was a bottle of lavender oil nearby, a type formulated for absorption into dragon scales, and I took it carefully, pouring a dollop, thick enough to balance there, on to the tip of a finger. I didn't need to use much, not in one go, not as I used the lavender oil to add a light tickle of a scent to the air. Something prickled at my nostrils and, with a second glance at the bottle, I realised that there was a touch of ginger in there too.

That was perfect. My mistress deserved the best, always the best.

She murmured, her feet relaxing in my hands, though, when massaging the oil into her scales, I could only focus on one at a time. I worked the oil across her sole, smoothing away the tension, even between the toes, soothing and gently caressing. Even the base of her claws, where they connected to her toes – everything deserved the utmost level of attention that I could pay. There was nothing else for me, nothing else at all that I would have rather been doing, only serving her.

It was only a shame, at least in my eyes, that there was the need for work in the world, for I would have been a very willing slave indeed as I massaged her feet, rubbing softly over the top, though I had to do it by feel. There were fine bones there – nothing I could injure accidentally with my hands alone, though I still wanted to take great care with Mistress Onyx, as much as she took care of me. Even though I was the slave and she was the mistress, she still took care of me and my needs, treating me as a treasured slave.

The dragoness rumbled and I tried to please her even more, digging my thumbs into her heels, seeking out the tension there and sweeping it away. I had to do it, had to see her through, kissing her toes, my tongue lapping at her claws, though it was just as well that they were blunt. I would have risked any manner of sharpness to please her and her glorious feet, of course, but I could still be grateful for little things like that.

She murmured and I followed her lead as she sat up, lifting one leg so that it was crossed over the other. I knew that position and scrambled to obey, up on my knees, but always on a lower level than her, cradling the offered foot in my hands. I bowed my head to kiss it, worshipping her, praising her, kissing each toe, over the top, close up where her foot connected to her ankle, her scales so fine there. I knew how tough the scales of her feet were, despite everything, and took more of the lavender oil again, as eager as ever in to serve.

"Mmm…"

I shivered, not daring to look up, not even as Mistress Onyx paid more mind to me, her tail curling back and forth. Even though I knew she was naked, I couldn't even look up at her, for I had not been given permission to look at her.

No. Better to slide my fingers between her toes and drag them back out and down the underside of her foot, down the sole, to the heel. I needed her, to please her, my world narrowing, her feet filling my vision. She swapped one foot for the other, placing the right one delicately in my hands, and I treated it just the same, working the oil in tenderly, devotedly, ensuring that there was not a drop of tension left in them, even as I pressed my nose to her foot and adoringly inhaled.

"Lie down, foot slave."

I scurried to obey, cock throbbing, but I did not expect her to walk her feet over me. Shivering in place, cock aching, I moaned, embarrassed by how easy it was for her to turn me on, to make me want her even more, always more. I never thought that it would ever be possible for her to turn me on any more than she was in any given moment – and yet Mistress Onyx surprised me each and every time.

Though it was not for me to say anything, her foot slave, nothing more than a foot servant and a footrest, anything that the dominant dragoness wanted from me. She walked her toes down my body to my cock, my breath held, barely believing that she was going to be so kind to me. And yet Mistress Onyx was always kind: a hard mistress who demanded a lot from me, but one that knew when to reward a slave too.

"Ohhhh… Thank you, mistress, oh…thank you."

She smirked, not sparing me any words, but that was for her to choose, one way or the other. All I had to do was to serve her, to do all that she wanted, even as she folded her feet around my cock one on either side, easily dwarfing my moderate cock. Size didn't matter there – it was not as if I was ever going to fuck her anyway. That was not for a slave to do, but it was a means to rewarding me, my heart surging, blood rushing to all the right parts of my body. I whined and whimpered, squirming in place, though stayed obediently there as she, once again, gave my cock a foot job that made all other thoughts slip from my mind.

Nothing else existed, only sensation, eyes fixed on her feet, how they twitched and flexed, pulling into a more comfortable position around my cock, though it was not as if it was going to take me long to blow my load anyway. She was too hot, too sexy, too powerful. And I just a servant to her, a willing, wanting dragon slave, whimpering with lust for her, the dragoness of my dreams.

I was only lucky to be there, right there where I was, her feet massaging my cock, pulsing and twitching around it, though I would never quite know how she managed to move her feet in that way. Maybe it was the squeeze of them, adding pressure and then taking it away again? I didn't know, didn't need to know, not as she worked me closer and closer to the edge, breath catching, eyes half-closed with passion.

Yet I couldn't help it as I cried out, spending my seed, weak spurts of cum dribbling out over her feet, marking her toes, standing out against her black, only just cleaned scales. And yet I couldn't stop myself, not even as she made a show of smirking and lifting her foot, wriggling her toes to show me what a mess I had made of her feet.

"Lick it off, slave."

Obediently, I scrambled to obey, tongue already out, wanting to let her know that I was there for her, that I would always be her little obedient foot slave slut, whatever she wanted, for however long she wanted. I sucked my own cum off her toes as if it was the finest treat in the world. For me, it was – all because it had come from Mistress Onyx's orders and involved her beautiful, strong, flexible feet.

It was there, sucking at her toes, lapping cautiously down the side of her foot to clean her scales with my tongue, that I found myself in my happy place.

There was nowhere else that I would rather be.

Not ever.

Healing Love

"N-no… No, you can't be… Emilia, please, hold on…"

The drake pored over his love, the dragoness sprawled out on the ground before him, blood speckling her scales. Gabriel nuzzled her, her pink scales adorned in such a way that should never have been seen before his eyes, the drake's dark tail sweeping back and forth through the sand. The storm rumbled above, but the dragoness that she had fought off, all for him, had turned tail and fled, unwilling to face Emilia's might.

Her wounds were grievous, damp sand clinging to her scales as the storm grumbled too close for comfort, though Gabriel's healing magic flowed softly over her. Pink waves of energy curled around her limbs where she had been injured, though whether it was a strain or a sprain, a cut or a broken bone, Gabriel's magic was more than adequate to see her to rights once more.

He murmured softly, flicking his tail, disliking her state, that she had done it for him.

"Emilia, you can't do this, you'll hurt yourself too badly one day," he whispered, snout tight with emotion. "I don't want to lose you. Why? Why do you do this? Leave it… There is no sense in this violence…"

But Emilia could not promise her lover something that she had no intention of giving, not when her heart burned fiercely for him.

"I did it…" She breathed. "All for you… Gabriel."

He looked up, tears in his eyes, sparkling on his cheeks.

"Darling, she was going to go eventually, you don't always need to leap to my aid…"

And yet she knew that she always would, the fire in her heart burning too brightly for him to ever be held back, the only dragon that she had ever fallen, quite literally, out of the sky for. Gabriel had caught her unawares that very first day she'd met him, veering off-course at the flash of his dark scales cutting through the sky, the silver sparkles that adorned him like stars. Yet Emilia would only learn later that those were best appreciated in the quiet solitude of a warm cave together, preferably before a crackling fire.

Where she should have been sweetness and light, Gabriel was only one-third of her size and she could not help but defend him, regardless of the dragon that sought his attention. They thought they could push him around, just because of his size, the hierarchy of different flights of dragons always changing, but she would not have that. Linking her tail with his and feeling better than she had since the last time he had infused her with his healing magic, more powerful in herself once more, she crooned to him.

"Gabriel..." She purred, eyes dancing, tongue flickering out over the pink scales of her lips, her horns catching the light from outside as evening pulled at the sky. "Will you not lay with me? I am the victor, after all, and it is only right that I should receive the spoils of my suitor..."

Gabriel sighed, though she caught the tiniest of smiles pulling at his lips, as if he couldn't quite hold it back in her presence. He checked her over for further injuries without comment, though stayed closer. That was all Emilia needed to know to shift in further, purring as she rubbed her body against his, standing as if to show by just how much she dwarfed him. With a little chirp that sent her heart fluttering in all the best ways, Gabriel shivered in place.

"Light the fire, darling."

She directed him softly, gently, as if it was the most natural thing in the world, yet there was no need for roughness in their relationship. That came outside, a side of Emilia that she had to draw into play, all to ensure that her lover remained safe. It was a big, bad world out there and it could be said that Gabriel had forgotten where the difficulties could lie after his time with her, as warm through as she already was for him. He was too sweet, too innocent, and all she wanted to do was to make sure that no one gave him the trouble he faced before, all so he could enjoy his life, with her, with his friends, studying magic... Doing all it was that his little heart desired.

Emilia was only glad that she was part of it and his life as she nuzzled down his back, snaking her tongue between the small, silvery spines, oh so light and delicate, just like the rest of Gabriel. He sent a spark to the fire pit in the centre of the cave to illuminate it in a blue, crackling blaze, the flames unnatural and yet inherently draconian, speaking of their own brand of magic. Emilia could have had and used that magic too if she had chosen to train it, but her strong, young, muscled body ached for more physical endeavours.

Still, his jaws parted willingly as she kissed him, drawing him against her as she sat back on her haunches, purring into his muzzle. The more dominant dragoness' tongue wove into his mouth and around his tongue, having explored every last inch of his muzzle already over the time they had been together. There was no secret as to their lust and their love, yet Gabriel still squirmed away from the open mouth of the cave, allowing anyone who was passing to see in, whimpering when she held him fast.

There was no risk of discovery, at least to Emilia, adoring Gabriel's shyer sensibilities, yet she wanted her sweet little drake right there and then. There was no time to move to darker, more private recesses of the cave, not when her heart pounded for him, her tail trying to flick as a deeply seated need tugged under her tail, where the vent of her sex was located. Already, his cock hardened, slipping from the slit at the base of his belly, a good size for her to toy with. Although Gabriel's little trick of swirling and flicking his tongue teasingly up against that spot at the roof of her mouth was almost enough to make her see stars.

"Mmm," Emilia groaned, separating, only briefly. "You're trying to distract me, darling… Lay back now, there's a good little draggie. I've got to make sure you're treated right, that there's not a scale out of place on your cute little body."

Gabriel shivered. It was too much when she talked to him like that, shivering, melting, becoming a puddle of loving lust for her, putty in her claws. For there was little more that he could have possibly wanted in the world than Emilia looming over him with a grin pulling at her lips, showing off her sharp teeth while he was left to be so small, so insignificant (but not also, at the same time) under her.

He moaned, head falling back a little more, horns tapping the hard ground, as her lips brushed his cock, teasing him, showing him a fragment of what was to come. They parted around the head of his cock, lightly tapered to a point with a defined head, suckling gently, her tongue lashing the length. It should really have been too much stimulation, all at once, for Gabriel, yet the smaller drake ground his teeth and groaned through them, tail flicking back and forth helplessly, bearing through it. Yet, before her, all he wanted to be was helpless.

Because he was safe there. He could trust her, show Emilia every last one of his vulnerabilities, even as her sharp teeth moved tenderly over his cock, making sure not to graze him. As dominant as she was, she was gentle, never the sort of dragoness who needed to raise her voice with him to control. Yet it was that control that had started the very rhythm of their days and nights and lives together, a flow that never once needed to be quelled.

Not when it suited them so perfectly.

Her tongue wrapped around his cock, caressing the length, her muzzle easily covering him – though that was not what they wanted. It was not the crème de la crème of their bodies coming together, twisting and writhing in dragon passion, but it was something close, something teasing, something that had his cock hard and throbbing. One thing that Emilia had worked out about Gabriel early on had been that his cock dripped and drooled easily, as if he simply could not contain himself, producing more pre-cum than would ever be necessary to slide into a partner.

Yet his dominant lover adored the expression of his lust, something that his body could not contain, as she moved over him, slurping down the taste of him on her lips, drops of pre-cum lingering in the base of her mouth, between her teeth. She purred and locked her lips with his again, even though it put Emilia's neck at a weird angle, forced to bend too much, using the tip of her tail to help position his cock for her vent. Nothing about mating in such a position with her on top and squatting over him was easy, yet it was her favourite for the position of control it so easily put her into, taking his length deep as she sank on to him.

They moaned, Gabriel's tongue fluttering weakly into her mouth, though Emilia lovingly held it as if it was his paw, her vent rippling around him, her inner muscular control greater than it had any right to be. He fit with her perfectly, her vent closing around him tightly, massaging his cock while her little drake lover whimpered into her mouth. Emilia trembled. Oh, she would do anything to have those adorable little whimpers from him for the rest of their lives. And, if she had her way about it, and Gabriel too, they would.

No words were needed as she took him, breeding him, stealing his seed. Oh, they had had all manner of dominant, kinky roleplays in the past, though that time was only for him and her, the pair above all else. Passion swelled between them, music in the frenzied beating of their hearts, Emilia rumbling a growl as her tail swept across the bare cave floor. The crackling of the flames drove them on, though there was nothing Gabriel could do, sprawled under her, even his wings trapped under his body.

He was her healer while she was his saviour. Together, they complemented each other. They could as for no more than that, not as his shaft throbbed eagerly within her, too keen to spill his seed already. There was no telling how quickly or slowly time passed when they were together, caught up in the moment as if time ceased to have any meaning at all, sharing breaths and grunted moans. His shaft throbbed inside her, aching for release, though Emilia kept him on the edge for what felt like hours, though Gabriel was sure that nowhere near that long could have passed.

How was he to tell? The drake didn't care when he was with her... He couldn't care, not with the heat of her scales against him, the tightness of her passage, how she didn't even have to move at all on top of him, letting the pull and tug of her inner muscles do the work for both of them. She milked his cock of everything he had to give until the drake trembled on the edge of passion, breaking the one-sided kiss and whining, burying his muzzle, shaking against his neck.

"Mmmph, yes, please, I need it, want it, want you," he babbled, near incoherent with lust, trembling all over without an ounce of self-control. "Yes, Emilia, darling, please, make me, I need, I want, I need, I want…"

Yet he could not get out the rest of his words as she swept a wing under him, cradling the smaller drake to her as she climaxed with a low groan, finally bearing down enough in the slickening mess of her sex for him to get off too. Gabriel gasped, awash in pleasure, his internally held testes spilling every drop of lust and love he held for her, though there would always be more for Emilia, so very much more. He moaned and twisted his head, striving to relieve a little more of the tension, yet his dominant lover held him there, letting him ride out the wave of climax.

Together, they rested, close and warm, the fire crackling. They needed nothing more than that, regaining their breath in the aftermath of the first round, close and warm in healing love.

She defended. He healed. Together, they made one another whole. And that was all the dragons needed, even with his cream trickling from her slit.

Emilia rumbled, eyes glinting with need.

The night was far from done yet as Gabriel showed her exactly how much she meant to him…

Spa Seduction

It had been a long, hard winter for a mare, the kind of winter that seemed to drag on forever in mud and rain and wind and snow. It was not easy for someone who rather enjoyed being outside in better times and, frankly, had set up her life so that she could be outside as much as possible. But Amethyst, sometimes, needed a few creature comforts of her own, a red mare with her mane and tail loosely braided as she stood on the steps of the countryside spa.

"Finally…"

She exhaled, a light bag hitched up on her shoulder, mountains rising behind the spa building, which had the external appearance of being made out of timber, though it was surely a modern, well-insulated construct. Amethyst, however, didn't really care, ears twitching and her braided tail swishing lightly against the backs of her legs, the cool spring air nipping at her coat. She could be curious about the structure at another time, when she explored over her weekend there before her colt joined her, when her body wasn't aching for a massage.

Everything was taken care of inside the spa, though it happened as in a blur, a kind stoat coming to take her bag, even though she was more than capable of carrying it herself, the receptionist checking her in with a smile that, for once, appeared to be genuine. Still, she didn't want to force anything or be an imposition at the mountain retreat, a break from reality that, even then, was so very sorely needed. The mare would have been more than happy to spend a few days relaxing in the pools, the sauna and the steam room, though she'd heard there were other facilities on offer there too.

Amethyst smirked, lips quirking as amusement played across them. Well, there were most certainly other services at the spa and, if all had gone to plan already, one of them would be waiting at her room. Now that was someone at the spa hotel that she was more than willing to take advantage of!

They'd offered themselves, after all.

And there they were, kneeling and bound on the floor of her hotel room, a stallion anthro with a glowing, golden palomino coat and a pure white mane and tail that spilt down his body as if they had been especially combed out. A perfectly oiled leather bridle clasped his head gently, though the bit in his mouth had been swapped for a hard, rubber ball gag, the type of gag that one could really dig their teeth into without worrying about harm either to the device or their jaw.

"Oh, aren't you lovely..."

She murmured to herself, walking around him, taking in how his arms were tugged lightly behind him, his body, down to his lower stomach, trussed up in a black leather harness that stood out against his light-coloured coat. The harness came with silver, metal fixings and O-rings that connected each strap perfectly, buckles gleaming, his arms able to be locked slightly behind him to the harness so that his shoulder blades were not pulled too much, all the while still reminding him of his restriction.

A rein that would not have been used on a non-consenting non-anthro equine hooked to the rings of the bridle, where the gag sat at the corners of his lips, two links of leather looping down to his chest. It was a means of control, forcing him to put a beautiful arch into his neck, though it was the kind of bondage that stopped him from lifting his head, restricting him even further, a bondage that, of course, had to be consented to.

His knees were forced apart with a spreader bar, but the most delicious part of that particular part of her stay there was how his balls and sheath were exposed, the former of which hung between his spread knees. His fetlocks and hooves had been left free, thicker as if there was a coat of feather there, some draft horse in his heritage, but his shaft had been forced from his sheath with a cock ring around the base, preventing it from retreating. The mare's eyes gleamed. Just as she liked it. Held there for her attention and no more than that, not permitted to attain pleasure or relief, not when she had so much more to take from him.

"I think you'll do nicely…for a start."

She cast off her T-shirt and shorts, the comfortable clothes that she had worn for travelling, a low, satisfied hum rising from her throat. Her colt could wait, for he would not be long after her, she was sure of it, even if he was due to arrive at the spa later that day. Tugging the golden palomino to the bed, only so that she had something there to steady herself, she propped a hoof up on the bed with a grin, revealing her bare sex to the equine, her underwear tangled up in the shorts that she had already slipped off. In nothing more than her chestnut coat of hair, a white diamond in the centre of her forehead, she could take everything she willed and more.

The stallion grunted, his tail flicking across the floor lightly behind him, the soft carpet plush, at least, for him to kneel on. Her sex teased lightly across the front of the ball gag, smearing her juices and scent into his nose, up close to his nostrils while they fluttered and puffed with short, sharp breaths, dragging all the air needed into his lungs that way. But the stallion had no say and neither did he want any say as the ball gag was removed, a passive player in how he was used, working his jaw only briefly before her sex pressed insistently to his lips.

He knew his job well, however, even if he was not to give her his name, all of the anthros servicing others at the spa there well-trained and anonymous. It was to protect them, though Amethyst did not consider that too deeply, winding her fingers through his mane to draw him in closer, his tongue snaking out expertly to kiss her folds.

"Oh, yes…"

She might not have been lying back on the bed, but having a spa slave there before her in bondage added an extra spicy edge to everything that she needed more than a long, slow orgasm. Sometimes the quick and the furtive came with even more desire tangled up in it, mumbling sweetness under her breath, her ears twitching back and forth, though she had everything right there before her that she needed at that time. Only the teasing laps of his tongue, pressing between her folds, drew her lightly back to reality, a pleasurable warming of reality that seared through her entire body in the very best of ways.

Groaning, she rolled her head back, the exposure of her bare throat hardly vulnerable, not when she so casually held such a position of power. His tongue pressed into her, seeking out her sensitive spots, yet he found them without any trouble at all, his skill showing through. Under no illusion that hers was the first pussy that the stallion had eaten out that day, she leaned back a little, rolling her hips up to meet the tantalising strokes of his tongue, simply in it to enjoy the ride.

"Ohhh… Mmmm…"

She didn't have to hold back, for she was sure that no sounds would filter through the heavy hotel room door to the hallway beyond – besides, it was part of what the spa offered. If they did not expect to hear some sex noises, they wouldn't have made it a key feature of the spa, even down to the kink dungeon and private play rooms that could be hired out below the ground floor. With the spa being set over multiple levels, she was particularly interested in the one that had a St Andrew's Cross set up with a full-wall window looking out over a waterfall. The reflections and ambiance… Mmm…

Some things were worth paying a little extra money for.

The stallion lapped deeply, fingers twitching as if he wanted to tease them up inside her too, though they were trapped behind him, helpless if not useless. He compensated with his tongue, his mane messed up where she twisted her fingers into it, holding him exactly where she wanted him, sweeping it deeply up inside, practically trembling against her. One tiny sensation was difficult to differentiate from any other, though the mare languished right where she was, skin prickling with heat, her dock flicking up as the braid of her tail twisted to the side in a whish of thick hair.

"Mmm…Yes… Come on, there's a good boy…"

He moaned against her at the praise and she encouraged him even more, pulling him against her, fingers griping tightly, though she did not need to release him, not in the slightest. With a low groan, she allowed every drop of pleasure to flow through her, whisper by whisper, until it built to a burning crescendo, her sex soaked, whinnying shrilly.

Yet what need did she have for self-control when she was already right where she wanted to be, getting the best start ever to her holiday? Amethyst's ears splayed out lustfully as she let her high take her, skin prickling, aching through as if it curled up more deeply inside her than ever, panting heavily through her nostrils. The stallion grunted, eagerly eating her out, his tongue flicking up against and again, lips closing around her clit where they had already been rubbing against her nub even as he lapped. Her juices trickled down his chin, thin and dribbling, yet he tried his best, even then, to lap up everything he could reach, tail flicking back and forth like a colt who was best suited to being down on his knees.

The air was quiet in the hotel room, bar her softening breaths, regaining lost air into her lungs, and the wet slurp of his tongue pulling along her slick flesh. She huffed hotly, ears flicking, running her fingers through his mane, though it did not lie as prettily down his neck as it had before, the scent of sex hanging in the air, tainted by a tickle of sweat. The mare smirked, running her fingers down his face. He had a thin stripe of white down the front of his head, something that she hadn't noticed before. To be fair to Amethyst, she had been a little preoccupied…

"Not a bad start… See to it that you're here tomorrow evening also, at eight. I have someone who might well want to meet you…"

But, for the moment, she was done with him. There was no need for pillow talk with a consensual spa slave nor any need for sweet moments as there would be someone along to take care of him in due course, she was confident of that. Gathering a fresh change of clothes, a robe and a towel, along with her swim wear, she made her way down to the spa on the ground floor, boasting an indoor and an outdoor pool that she was *dying* to try out.

It was something new for her not to have to worry about anything, to go from one moment to the next without fussing, without fretting, without thinking that she had some work to do, that there was someone, something, somewhere that needed her attention. There, she was anonymous, not someone who could deliver something to the spa staff, just another patron, even if they did, of course, know her by name. With it being such an exclusive location with a hefty price tag attached, every need was catered for. All she had to do was enjoy.

And wasn't that a luxury?

They greeted her warmly at the entrance to the leisure facilities, though she skipped the gym that time. She'd done more than enough work to warrant a break, looking to soothe, to recover, not work out her muscles even more. Cardio too, most certainly, could wait: not her favourite activity by far, unless it involved the bedroom. She donned a simple bikini, strapless over the chest with bottoms cut to show off her best features, and stepped lightly out to the pool, her mane and tail out of their braids, flowing freely down her body with a light curl to them. A towel was set aside for later, the mare plunging deep into the water.

It was not deep, to be fair, but enough that she could not feel the bottom at the deep end, striking out into a backstroke, enjoying the flow of the cool water, not too warm, not too cold, around her ears, how her mane tickled her body as it flowed down. It was just right, everything perfect, and she took her time, allowing everything to come exactly as it was intended to. There were others in the pool too, of course, but those with staff lanyards around their necks were of the most interest to her. Everyone else would just need to be a bystander, watching, or perhaps she could even play the part of the voyeur. On certain days and hours, of which she was covered by, the spa itself could be used for more adult activities too.

Drawing herself from the pool, looking for the steam room, she caught the eye of a small, light Arctic fox, his fur dry and brushed, so fluffy that there was a part of her that ached to run her fingers through it. The ceiling of the pool stretched overhead in a line of sheer glass, sunshine glancing through, warming her coat, though she grazed her eyes with his only briefly. She didn't need any more than that.

The steam room beckoned, the wet, clinging heat soothing the aches and pains from her body, leaning back on the smooth bench as the glass door closed behind her, keeping as much heat as possible trapped in there with her.

"Mmm..."

Alone, she relaxed, thinking of the tensions held in her body, letting them be free, one by one. It was a shame that it was the kind of spa where one was still expected to be wearing clothing, or covered up outside the changing rooms, but that didn't mean that she didn't want to enjoy every benefit it had to offer. Maybe if she visited the sauna, she'd have to ensure that she had a towel around her only, which was more easily disposed of for cleaning, more hygienic in her opinion. The steam room sank into her body, however, deeply resting her muscles, though she barely perked her ear when the door opened.

"A little fox said that you might like some company..."

It was not the fox that she had teased with a sway of her hips but a taller cheetah, his tail swinging behind him, an easy grin on his lips, though his whiskers quivered. Amethyst was almost too relaxed to take him up on his offer, but the soft, heavy heat of the steam room begged a slower kind of lust entirely.

"Come here," she all but purred, crooking her finger in the direction of the sultry feline, so slim and powerful in his coiled glory. "Sit. I think you can help me relax some..."

He sat as the horse bid, sliding down his loose shorts, though Amethyst was sure that the spa employees had more than enough changes of clothing at the resort to last them a lifetime if anything became destroyed or torn off in a fit of passion. The cheetah's cock was quick to rise to attention, lightly barbed but softly so with no sharpness to the thicker, plumper spines, cock that begged attention. Yet that was the very thing that the cheetah was there to give her as the mare tugged her bikini bottoms to the side, not even bothering to disrobe as she presented her already slick folds to the tapered head of his cock.

No words were needed, not as she sank on to him, taking him deep, not caring for the hardness of the bench, a tingle of eucalyptus in the air. She moaned, letting her nose tip forward, the feline purring, tail flicking, the dark rosettes of spots standing out from his brighter fur, the bulk of his body. Her hands ran down his chest, feeling the firm, functional muscle there, not an ounce of spare fat on the cheetah, even though she could not feel his ribs without pressing, not through his covering coat of fur.

"Mmm..."

They moaned, rolling their hips together in ecstasy, the cheetah spearing lightly up into her, though there was no rush to their lust, taking their time, allowing passion to rise exactly as and when it was desired. It needed to be no more than what it was as steam floated around them, the air stirred up by even the light movement of their bodies coming together, her sex squeezing around him, a delightful glint in her eye. It was a small movement, a subtle little thing, the soft barbs raking through her passage every time she rose from his cock, though the cheetah's shaft filled her nicely.

It was a good moment, one that would linger in her mind for long after it passed, the cheetah staff member dipping his head to sensually kiss and nuzzle at her breasts, having tugged her strapless bikini top down under them to have full access. Even the light tickling of his whiskers had her quivering, the mare catching her breath, groaning deeply up in the back of her throat, tail flicking back and forth. It swung more heavily, the hairs clinging together with moisture still lingering from the pool, for only so much wringing out of the long flow of hair could be done before slipping into the steam room after a rinse off in the shower. The cheetah did not seem to mind as it swung against his legs, pulling at her nipples, one after the other, catching them between his lips and grazing them, ever so gently, with his teeth.

It was the mark of a predator, the sharp flush that a prey anthro simply could not bring to the table. And yet it was still the mare who was in control, flashing him a devious grin, her fingers curling, tightly, around his shoulder. Her hips rocked more fervently, interested in her own pleasure, though from the huffing pants the feline gave too, it seemed that he was coming closer and closer to his own high.

"Can you hold off?" She breathed, arching her back for a touch of different sensation, pressing his cock up against her G-spot, holding down a grunt. "Mmm... With that view, I doubt it..."

With his head tipped the way it was, her breasts filled his vision, the pink of her nipples showing through her chestnut fur, the cheetah moaning softly. Yet he was only there to serve, shivering under her despite the heat of the steam room, a body moving past the door but nobody disturbing them. Not that it would have mattered if anyone walked in on them, but Amethyst rather preferred having her partners completely to herself until she was done with them. Some would say she was jealous like that, though all she knew was that she knew what she wanted. To her, that would never be a bad thing.

But he could not hold off, forced to push his paw urgently down between their bodies to at least attempt to bring Amethyst off first, the mare's smirk coming with a flush of pride. Oh, she liked that she could rile even the spa staff up to such a point that their skill and training wavered, though she had not really done anything much at all. It was all in the attitude, though there was surely a wide variety of patrons, from all walks of life, frequenting the spa.

His fingers played with her clit expertly, pressing down for a little wider pressure as to the flesh around her nub, squeezing and circling, letting soft tremors ease into her body. The need to climax built and built as she ground her hips against him, allowing the cheetah to take her there, a low yowl breaking his lips in the moment before she claimed his lips with hers.

Kissing him deeply, she pinned him back to the hard bench, the smooth back of it providing an ample rest for him, as much as her knees ached. With the heavy heat wrapped around them, it was a little more difficult to breathe than either may have liked, but they would not be there for all that much longer as he grunted and pressed against her, shoulders shuddering with need. His tongue tangled with hers, but it was the mare who easily dominated, bearing his tongue down with hers as she took her chance to explore his muzzle, even brushing her tongue against his sharper, feline teeth.

Neither could have said which one of them got off first, but it was close enough that it could have been said to be together in the sultry heat, the mare tensing, bearing down, the short claws of his free paw finding her hip and digging in sharply. The flesh of sensation pulsed through her as orgasm gripped her, the pull of her sex wrapped around his aching shaft, pushing deep inside her as she sank down, refusing to allow any part of his cock to remain outside her pussy in her moment of need.

Their orgasms dragged out, his seed flowing up inside her, slickening the tightness of her passage around his cock, though there were no more thrusts to come. Her bikini bottoms clung to the side of his shaft, but neither noticed, kissing passionately, nostrils flaring and puckering as they drew in what breath they could, a little light-headed.

Amethyst moaned into his mouth, drawing back slowly, sleepily, her eyelids heavy.

"Mmm… That was very nice. Are all the cats here as quick to take a lady as you are?"

The cheetah's jaw dropped, stammering, blushing, even when he should have been well used to such teasing, Amethyst's chuckle staying with him as the mare tugged her attire back into place and bid adieu to the steam room. It was time for a break and, dressed appropriately once more, she grumbled at the need to slip into the shower to rinse off the sweat from her body before dropping into the plunge pool.

Cold water enveloped her, surprising after the heat of the steam room, and she grit her teeth, stifling a gasp at the cold, as invigorating as it was. They were an acquired taste, to be fair, though she wanted to experience more, awake and ready, even as the afterglow of lust tingled through her.

There was more still to experience at the spa, leaving the leisure area for the time being and heading to a massage that she had been told was pre-scheduled for her. That one was a surprise, though her mind mused over it as she patted her coat dry, brushing out her hair and blowing drying it in nothing but her bare coat in the changing rooms. Perhaps she would have a stud, someone who could do a nice, deep tissue massage, or maybe it would be softer, sweeter, with aromatherapy. There were even hot stone massages on offer too and she wondered what one of those would be like, the heat of the stones sinking into her, giving her the impression that they were much heavier than they actually were, pinning her to an imagined massage table.

But she would see who would be there to take care of her and she was sure that, once again, the spa and the service offered would deliver everything she could have wanted.

Amethyst wasn't disappointed. Ascending the stairs to the private treatment room, nude but for the long, white robe that covered her modesty, she entered a softly lit room with light music playing with a stag, not heavily muscled and not skinny but perfectly in the middle, holding the door open for her.

"After you, ma'am," he murmured, a tilt to his head, a full rack of antlers tapping against the wall behind him as he allowed her space. "We have a very special treatment set up for you today, all set to the preferences outlined when you made your booking. Unless you have any special requests?"

She smiled, letting him take her hand and kiss it, a charmer who was good at what he did, though she only hoped that he was as good with his hands and tongue as he was his words. That he was only wearing the typical black pair of shorts required for most male staff members there helped too, a nice bulge promising a good time, if that was the way that things were to go.

"I'd rather see what you have in mind," she murmured silkily, running her fingers up his chest and pushing his jaw up lightly as she tugged her hand back from his. "Impress me."

He stuttered, eyes widening a fraction, caught on the back hoof, though he tried to follow through quickly, sweeping into the room, a little more rushed than he would otherwise have been. And, just like that, Amethyst had the power back where it belonged in her hands, sure that she would get everything she wanted there and more.

She laid herself down, allowing him to slip the robe from her shoulders, comfortable in her nudity. No towel was needed and she waved him off with a smile, flicking her tail to the side as she laid face-down with her nose through the padded, lavender-scented hole in the massage table.

And, oh, how he impressed her, hands sweeping down her back, soothing muscle that had been sore for too long, overworked for too long, working heat into her body first so that she was even more pliable, at least for her massage, under his hands. There were no such things as knots that needed to be worked out, but there were contractions in her muscles from where she had held herself protectively, overworking and working in bad posture. Not everything could be fixed in a short amount of time, but it could most certainly be eased as she melted under his expert hands.

Soon enough, however, the stag's hands worked lower and lower, easing over her glutes and kneading deep into her backside in a way that was not purely work, not that kind of professional. It could have been, under different circumstances, but she flicked her tail against his hands, teasingly draping it where the hair dried.

The stag shivered, working down the backs of her legs, coming in closer and closer, yet the cord of tension that linked them strung out tighter and tighter. It had to break, sooner or later, but both mare and stag were willing to see what it could be played into first of all, Amethyst shifting slightly to maintain her comfort, the familiar stirring of need rising in the pit of her stomach.

He showed his true colours, however, almost climbing up on the table behind her and parting her rear cheeks with his hands. Before the equine could even take another breath, his muzzle shoved between her cheeks, tongue out and flickering over her tail hole, the tight pucker of flesh there, in a tenacious dance.

"Mmmph…"

She tightened her hand into a fist, tensing up, but in a good way. It was difficult to hold too much tension in her body when his tongue delved into her tail hole, tracing around the pucker and pushing back in, keeping her guessing as to what he would do next. Pleasure tingled through her, though he kept more to the sensitive ring of flesh rather than trying to lap deeply up inside her. It was good, yet only a taste of more to come, rimming her tail hole with loving submission.

"Do you treat all your clients like this?" Amethyst teased, keeping the pant out of her voice. "Or just the ones you want to get on your knees for?"

She swore she could feel his blush as he tongued her hole, running around, even up under the dock of her tail while her body quivered. It brought with it a new kind of need, but the massage helped everything remain relaxed, rocking her weight lightly from left to right, from one hip to the other, but otherwise merely enjoying the attention that was being lavished upon her. There was little else that was needed, not as her tail flicked up, allowing him to stroke with his fingers around the sensitive base, the dock where so many tiny nerve endings were located.

He slipped down, licking his lips, her pussy glistening with a hint of her arousal, though it was not as if the mare was trying to hide it. His fingers slid into her, parting her folds and her sex for him, curling up inside her for her G-spot, though it took a few experimental strokes and twitches of his fingers before he caught exactly where it was. What would have taken less experienced males perhaps several sessions or more he caught on to swiftly, demonstrating his skill. Yet it was not skill without passion and Amethyst groaned, moving her legs apart a little more for him. Her clit pressed lightly into the padding of the massage table, though she was not in any position for his muzzle to work her over as she wanted, even if she was exactly in the position that she wanted to be in.

"Deeper, buck," she breathed, teasing, one ear flicking back to him as if he was not quite worth the attention of her turning her head. "Use those fingers… I thought I said to impress me?"

He grunted as if put out, though if he was ever so slightly riled up that would be even closer to getting her what she wanted out of everything. Amethyst grinned, rolling her hips back up on to all fours, though the stag moved away before she could take a touch more control, grinding on to his fingers and muzzle.

Ah, but he had something better in mind, adjusting the height of the table so that it came back down to roughly his hips, the bulge rising more stringently in the front of his black shorts. With a pointed look from the mare, he slipped out of them, kicking them off his cloven hooves where they would not get in the way, and she scooted back to the edge of the table, still lying on her front, but with her legs hanging over it, her pussy poised at the edge.

"Show me what you've got, buck, perhaps there's even a tip in it for you…"

He chuffed a laugh, taking his hardening cock in his hand, stroking it lightly, though it only took a couple of pumps to get it to full hardness.

"I don't work for tips, but you are making this a challenge."

That was just what made it all the more entertaining for her, letting him line up behind her, not honestly wanting to move all that much after her steam and her massage. Some would have called it topping from the bottom, but Amethyst called it "doing exactly what she wanted." It was something indeed to have a male penetrate her when she controlled every stroke, able to take the pleasure quite as if she was receiving a different kind of massage entirely.

And yet he surprised her, not presenting his cock to her pussy straight away but something smaller to her tail hole. Slick and lubricated, it eased into her backdoor entrance easily, stretching open the loosened pucker of flesh, a small plug that widened towards the middle to a nice stretch. Yet it was not as small as she grunted with the light strain, popping in easily to the neck of the plug once it was past that widest part.

"Mmm..."

Then and only then did she flick her tail to the side in open invitation, allowing the stag to mount her, his long, thick cock slipping inside her easily with all the preparation. Having another's hands on her got the mare hotter and readier than ever, moaning softly, taking every moment of pleasure that was offered to her, her head popping up from the table as she rested it on her arms instead.

His cock filled her perfectly with more of a stretch than the cheetah's shaft had given her as it pushed deep, the stag perfectly poised to please her with long, sensual rolls of his hips. He grunted out his need, nostrils quivering, yet she shot him a glance back, daring him to do more. She had said for him to impress her, after all, had she not?

She was not yet impressed, but she was due to be as her sex tightened around him, bringing him to a chuffing pant, his rack of antlers tilted as he drove on, need flooding his body. He thrust hard, hips bouncing off her backside with every stroke, though she spread her legs amenably, bare hooves digging into the flooring for purchase. She wasn't going anywhere and neither was the table she lay on, groaning softly, letting roll after roll of pleasure wash through her.

Yet it all ramped up another notch as he pressed to the base of the plug under her tail, vibrations travelling up inside her as the tightness of being filled in two holes at once strained through her entire body. Electric thrills tingled through her entire form, moaning aloud, twisting her head to the side to watch the stag lean over her, a line of desperation in his muzzle where she could see that he was trying harder than he had recently to please her.

It was good to see someone trying, her lips pulling up on one side with a smirk. But he had given her what she'd wanted and that was coming under her control: he didn't have to be trussed up and bound to do that. He only had to submit, to obey, to go beyond what the limits of merely doing his job were.

It didn't have to be just fun for the mare, after all.

She squeezed around him, deliberately letting her legs come a little closer together as orgasm rose, the pound of his cock pushing her closer and closer to the edge. Having a break between her climaxes helped her get there again swiftly, not having to worry at all about that pressure blending to strain, lingering solely in pleasure. That was a better place to be, Amethyst thought, gripping the table, rolling her hips back against him as the stag huffed and puffed, his soft-skinned balls bouncing off her body with every thrust.

Yet it was the mare who climaxed first with a devious whinny, shrill and high-pitched, conveying every drop of need that she did not need to hold back. All that she needed, all that she desired, coursed through her as ripples of pleasure escalated to waves. Her body contracted and her muscles pulled around the stag's cock and the butt plug alike. The delicious tightness ached through her as she arched her back, shoulder blades pushing back, heat tingling, simmering, needing every second of it.

It had to come down from such a high, however, leaving her with a full body, warming afterglow, grunting softly, her tail flicking back and forth against the stag's stomach. He eyed her up, licking his lips, but Amethyst, once more, caught him off-guard with a wave of her hand, pointing back.

He caught on to her meaning, separating from her, his cock sliding out with a lewd slop of her arousal, enough to coat his cock in a gleam of combined sexual fluids but not to drool in a messier cream-pie, which could have been the case if he had spent himself inside her. The mare groaned as she sat up, perched on the massage table, stretching her arms out over her head as the butt plug jostled inside her.

"Mmm… That was good. Best *massage* I've had in a while, buck."

She grinned, dropping him a wink as a blush rose to his cheeks, though the deer did not hide how he looked at her, still with the hunger of one who had not reached their own high in his eyes. But that wasn't Amethyst's problem, not even with his raging hard-on twitching faintly with the pump of blood within.

"I think that's all for me today. I'll see myself out."

Standing, she bent slightly to tug the butt plug out, relaxing as it pulled free, and set it on the table with a smile. As if everything she was doing was perfectly normal, the stag's ears perked forward to her, expecting more, she hummed a tune that only she knew to herself, a swing in her hips as she swept up her robe in one hand. That, unfortunately, would still be needed outside the treatment room. Still, she hoped there would be another treat waiting for her in her hotel room, whether her colt had made it to the spa or not.

"Uh…"

The stag shifted, standing as if he didn't know what to do, tail flicking, antlers accidentally rapping a shelf that he shuddered away from. She cast him a look, her arousal marking her inner thighs, hardly even pausing as she made for the door.

"Oh, were you expecting something more?"

Amethyst quirked an eyebrow, blowing the stag a kiss as she donned her robe. He let out a grunt as her body was, once again, covered up, his cock still hard, still leaking, his needs not quite met. Or, at least, not met in the way that he expected them to be, appearing smaller than her, despite his rack of antlers putting himself a good head and almost shoulders too above the mare physically. Control could do that to an anthro, though it was rare that it was savoured so sweetly.

"I'm sure I'll see you again…if you're good."

She left the stag to figure out what that meant, a smile on her lips and comfortably satisfied, at least for the time being. Maybe she'd come see him again or maybe she wouldn't – but she'd see, one way or another, how far he was prepared to enjoy the quiver in his legs, the need that made him want to drop before her, to please, to serve. It might be nothing at all, yet that was half the fun in playing her little games, everyone getting what they wanted, in the end.

Amethyst smiled.

The rest of her spa trip, especially after her partner arrived, was sure to be even better than how it had begun.

She'd make sure of it.

Her Bitch

"Head down, slut."

He quivered, the black Labrador shivering in place, though he had been under Mistress Steel's hard hoof many times before. In her play room, which could have been as innocuous as a spare bedroom if the grey mare had wanted it to be such, she was the queen, seated on a tall-backed throne with crimson, plush seating and a towering back of polished, dark wood. The canine did not know what wood it was actually made out of, though it was none of his concern, not as Mistress Steel crossed her legs, stealing even a slight glance of her latex-covered pussy from him.

What he did know was that his mistress was resplendent, fully secured in his submissive role, his tail lifted submissively as if to show off that every part of his body was hers and hers alone. He didn't need to do any more than that, never anything more than that, always hers, submissive and giving up everything to her. To her, he was Puppy Spot when he was in her play room, when the relationship between them changed to mistress and slave, however consensual it was, giving him space from reality and the pressure of making decisions.

If he was just there to serve, all as Puppy Spot, for the singular white spot on his rump, so small that an uncaring eye would have skimmed over, everything was okay with his world. He could focus solely on being pleasing, on submitting to her, on looking out for all the little things that he could do to be better for her. The smallest of things, after all, could be the most important.

Above him, Mistress Steel, otherwise known as Misty, tapped a whip against the palm of her opposite hand, though the smack of black leather into her hand did not hurt her, merely making a noise. Her attire had been carefully chosen that day with an under bust corset that pressed up her chest without hiding anything from view, her nipples on show, perky in the slightly cool air of the play room. Her short coat of grey hair was lightly dappled, jigging a black hoof in the air with her legs crossed, lips quirked up in a tiny smile, though her mane and tail were both neatly and tightly braided. That was something that Puppy Spot had done for her before they had gotten started, but the whip was yet to be used.

"Poor little puppy…"

The mare took her time with her words, confident in the sense that she had all the time in the world with him. And time did not have any meaning for the black lab either as he quivered there, his nose tipped down to the ground, kissing the hoof that remained by the throne on the carpet there, though the rest of the room was poured latex: smooth and easy to clean. Of course, it was always him that ended up cleaning, but it was a soothing final task to a session, to be fair, something that helped ground him and bring him back to reality again.

His backside, of course, was left shoved up in the air as the anthro dog hunkered down on his forearms, Spot resting his chin on the ground while she hummed lightly, as if to herself. And yet the mare knew, even on that small level, that she could draw the canine along with her with the slightest, softest of sounds, however she pleased. Everything she did, when they were in the play room together, was deliberate and calculated.

Except maybe her moans. He loved when he could push her that far, either with his tongue between her legs or worshipping other parts of her. Sometimes, Mistress Steel even let him "fuck" her with a strap-on, though his cock was never permitted to enter her pussy.

But that was alright, a bitch's cock didn't deserve to be the bone buried inside his mistress' pussy. If he was lucky, however, he would be made to serve her in a way that got his cock hard and throbbing, repressed sexual desire igniting within him like never before.

"Up. On the dais."

He knew what that meant. The walls of the play room were covered in shelves, covered in clear doors so that they were protected from dust, the interior illuminated to show off the many tools and toys and implements that she had to tease and torture him with. He moaned and nodded, crawling to the raised platform only a few feet away, illuminated in a soft spotlight. The control for the lights must have been in his mistress' hand, but it was not his place to ask questions. Although he had been in the play room many times over in his time with her, the rest of the room being cast into sultry, tempting darkness, certain areas only strategically illuminated, still made him shiver in barely contained lust.

"All fours. Don't look around."

He groaned, doing as she asked. He was fortunate that the raised dais, which put him at roughly hip height to her, was padded, for it was more comfortable than the hard floor at the best of times. It was a submissive position to hold too and Spot had to fight down the urge to dip his chest and raise his ass, wanting to do more.

Yet sometimes all he needed to do was exactly what his mistress wanted him to do, what she had ordered. Dimly, as he sank deeper into the sub-space that he had already had one paw in at the start of their session, he breathed slowly and evenly, letting his lungs expand to take in more and more air. It would be needed.

The rustle of something pulling over his mistress' short coat of grey hair and scuffing her latex underwear caught his attention, the dog unable to stop himself from perking up his ears. What was she putting on? He hadn't even realised that she had something else there with her, though perhaps the whip had been there to deliberately mislead him.

His shaft pushed out from his sheath, thinking of that whip again, how delectable the slap of it on his raised, exposed, vulnerable backside was. Oh, how he loved that, even though the blend of pleasure and pain was not for everyone. It got him harder than ever and he was almost disappointed that his mistress was not going to playfully punish him that day, even though there were many, many more things that he could do for her, that they could do together.

"Little bitch, I think you need reminding of your place," she murmured, hooves moving quietly over the rubber floor, though Puppy Spot did so enjoy how they clopped over the harder, wooden floors in the house too. "Don't you agree? No... I don't want an answer from you. I can speak for you when you are...otherwise disposed."

He didn't know what that meant – at least until she came around to his front, a smirk on her muzzle, the lines of her defined cheekbone and smile highlighted by the strategic lighting, making her look more dominant and dangerous still. The canine whimpered, wanting to tuck his tail down, though his eyes had already fixed on exactly what Mistress Steel wanted them to: the hard length of equine-cock-shaped dildo jutting from her crotch. It may not have been the biggest toy in her collection, but he knew it was one of the most comfortable for her to wear.

"Take it all, my bitch..."

She crooned darkly, feeding the cock into his mouth as he moaned around it, nodding weakly, doing as his mistress willed. Yes, that was what he was there for, all he was there for, everything that he had to do. Sucking a cock was not as fun as eating out her pussy, slurping up deep into her wetness to bring her to a shrieking rise of flaring pleasure, but it was still pleasuring her and that was the most important thing of all. Whatever that entailed…

For it was serving her that made his guts churn and his balls ache as if he was losing control – control that he had already, willingly and lovingly, placed into her dominant hands. With the heavy, thick collar around his neck, attention drawn to it, he grunted and wagged his tail, leaning a little more than before into the warm clasp of the leather. It was comforting, all in a good way, even as he slathered the faux cock in his own saliva, dragging and running his tongue around it, all so he could please her.

He had to serve and his mistress crooned above him even as the canine's eyes fell half-lidded, losing himself in the moment. He only needed to serve, to feel, comfortable there, slurping and sucking as if it was a real cock that could give his mistress even more direct pleasure too. The feel of the hard silicone in his muzzle was not enough to bring him back to that reality at all, bobbing his head on it, turning his head from the left to the right, all for a better angle, showing off his best cock sucking skills.

"Mmm…" She crooned, petting his head, though Mistress Steel, as always, was just a little bit too rough with him. "That's nice… What a good pup you can be…sometimes. But still my horny little bitch. I can see that dick of yours out and wagging, bitch, don't even try to hide it."

He whimpered and would have ducked his head if he had been able to, but he was too busy blowing her faux cock to do that, to ignore her direct command. Yes, his cock was out, throbbing, drooling, dripping, but he didn't think of it. He'd been denied release for so long at that point that to expect to be relieved of his need felt like something that, quite simply, was not going to come.

"Leave it."

He shuddered. That was a command that one might have given a real dog, but he obediently let the dildo slip from his maw, tongue rolling out as he panted heavily. His mistress seemed to be moving on more quickly than usual that day and the change of pace threw him off, which was precisely what she most likely intended. He could only speculate, but her intentions, very rarely, led to warm, soothing, comforting things for him. Spot would not have wanted that anyway.

He could have guessed that the toy was going to press into his rear, but Puppy Spot was grateful, even then, for the thin smear of lube that she gave the surface, adding it to the mess of his slick saliva. He had not been worked up, for it was what he preferred, though his mistress clearly wanted to get right down to it.

"Cry for me, bitch…"

He whined in his very best plaintive tone, shaking his head, rounding his shoulders and thrusting back to meet her, all as the cock pressed into him, deeper and deeper, stretching him open. It was only at his entrance for a breath of a moment, his mistress' hand closing around the base of his tail just to make sure that it was kept yanked up and out of the way, but it was enough.

Mistress Steel knew that he trembled for her, that he ached for her, that everything, every tiny motion of his body, was all for her. He tried to grind back against her, but the dominant mare gripped the base of his tail firmly, thrusting and grinding, driving in deeper and harder, rougher than ever, with every stroke. It hurt, not quite enough lube along the length of the faux cock, but he ached for more, to be humiliated, to be put in his place and forced to stay there, cock aching and throbbing, though he knew that he was not allowed to cum.

It stretched him out even as he strove with all his might to muffle the moans, clenching around the cock in his backside, head swimming with spinning passion. Mistress Steel most likely wouldn't even allow him to cum, though that was alright with him. It would only keep him coming back to her for more, whimpering and moaning, pleading with her to let him please her, to do something for her, to do anything for her. Anything at all that would let him be submissive to her, lusting and moaning the whole time. Unless she gagged him, of course.

"Such a slut… I can feel you squeezing around it, bitch. Isn't that all you are? A pathetic, cock-hungry bitch?"

"Ah!" He cried out, her hand connecting sharply with his backside, sending his sensitive flesh and muscle jiggling with the force of the slap. "Yes! Ah! Yes, Mistress Steel! Yes, Mistress!"

She rained down blows on him, dragging him back on to her faux cock with every rampant stroke, fucking him like there was nothing else in her mind, needing him, aching for him, though he was only there to serve her, to please her. He sank deeper into that softness of submission, letting it close around him, right where he was safe and secure, warm and comfortable in his sense of being. It didn't matter that his buttocks smarted and that the burning rise of pain was beginning to flare deeply through him, only that he was there where he needed to be, serving her, his tail hole straining around Mistress Steel's dick.

She thrust harder, faster, as if every stroke into his vulnerable anal passage was to punish him. Puppy Spot whined and whimpered, though tried to be quiet, for he didn't want his mistress to think that he was not amenable to what she was giving him, every bit of punishment and pleasure. It was all agreed, all consensual, and something that he yearned for, more and more, with every pump of that thick length inside him. It even warmed to the heat of his body as he grunted for more, to please her, squeezing hard around it even if that made things even more difficult for him.

And, still, his mistress was not satisfied. Or, at least, she made out that she wasn't, sending a delicious coil of dreaded heat through him when she paused, only half the dick buried in his backside.

"Pathetic performance..." She scoffed, flicking her tail as she dragged the toy from him, though Spot was only glad, in some small way, that he had not cum. "You disappoint me, slave."

That was okay, something that was agreed upon between them. Sure, her words came with a burning flare of humiliation, but, well...the arousal searing through him, as if a flame had been lit in the heart of his being was more than worth it. Panting heavily, he kept his head down, the soft padding under him cushioning his elbows and knees especially, his tail hole strained. Even though he could not look around, the heavy collar around his neck keeping his head in place, he swore the pucker was gaping, twitching faintly, even though he was sure too that all would tighten up again very quickly. If his mistress was not happy with his performance, he'd even be willing to take a bigger cock for her, all to see if there was a way, some way or the other, for him to please her.

She left his backside bare of her length as she drew away, the pup whimpering in the absence of her. Yet she only returned to her throne, sitting there with her legs spread and an imperious look in her eye.

"You have one more chance, bitch," she said, crooking her finger dispassionately in his direction. "Fuck yourself on my dick. No orgasm. You haven't earned anything like that yet."

He knew it, even as he crawled to her, standing only when he had to sit astride her lap. She hooked her fingers around his heavy, leather collar and the canine leaned hungrily into the restriction, the close control.

Oh, how he needed it... Even as he sank on to her cock as if it was the only thing in the world that he knew, that he wanted, that he yearned for. The rest of the room and even the world beyond the two of them no longer even existed for him, only serving her, riding her cock as he sat on her lap, pushed up on to the tips of his toes so that he could get the maximum height grinding up and down her hard length.

The dog could almost imagine that it was real too, that every clench and every twitch of his aching, stretched backside around her gave his mistress even more pleasure than before, heart pounding ruthlessly, raw need coursing through him like never before. His cock ached, hard and pointed directly at her, though his mistress didn't even give it a second glance, not even a touch.

It was beneath her attention.

He was beneath her attention.

And the puppy loved every sordid second of it.

He whimpered, rising and falling more and more fervently on her cock, his cock aching, drooling, pre-cum beading and spilling forth from the tip. Even that tiny sensation, the glisten of it thickening there and pouring down, was too much for him, forcing him to slow and pause, shaking his head, rolling it from one shoulder and back again, all to try and keep himself under control. But he didn't need to be under his own control, not while Mistress Steel had him held, quite firmly, in the palm of her paw, need rising, throbbing, lust tangled between them.

Yet there could never be any doubt in his mind that she was the dominant party, that she was the one that held his leash, that she was and would always be the one that he looked up to above all else. It was all that he needed, day by day and hour by hour, thrust by agonising thrust. It pushed deep up inside him, grinding over his prostate, that cock, forcing more and more little bubbles of pre-cum from the head of his dick. And yet the mare still wouldn't let him cum, still wouldn't even entertain the idea, smirking as she leaned back in her seat.

"Do you think you deserve it, bitch?" She said, stroking a finger ever so lightly up the length of his cock, though not enough to give Pup Spot the stimulation that he so sorely craved. "Do you think you deserve to spend your dirty load, your wasted seed? Of course, you do not. You never did."

She grinned, parting her lips as she dragged him in close, forcing him down all the way on to her dick. He grunted as it pressed up deep inside him, his cock aching, balanced too close to the edge of orgasm for any kind of comfort. Never again would there be comfort, not like that, not with her.

And he loved it.

"But maybe that worthless mouth of yours, slut, can be put to other uses. Oh, how you stare... But you're only good to serve. When you're trained. When you're disciplined. A pup like you comes with too many caveats."

She held his collar tightly, forcing him to ride her, harder and faster, his cock achingly hard. Oh, how he wanted to cum, but he could not, sweating profusely through the pads of his paws, knowing that he couldn't disappoint her. It took everything that he had in him to not cum right there and then, his tail hole aching, thighs burning.

All he had to think about was riding her cock, about pleasing her, about doing everything for the mare, Mistress Steel. She was all that mattered, even though the dog did not dare lock his gaze with hers. That would have been the utmost mark of disrespect and far, far from all that he felt from her.

"What a slutty pup," she crooned, licking her lips, actively drinking in the sight of him. "You want this... You want to be used... You want to have someone's attention on you, to feel seen. But you're just a slut that needs to be put in their place and kept there, at my hoof and on the end of my leash. Isn't that right, bitch?"

He moaned, tongue lolling out pinkly.

"Yes... Yes, Mistress," he forced out, though her gaze was raking down him again, attention distracted to her next focus. "I'm here...to please...to be used... I'm your...loving...unff...bitch... Nnggghhhh..."

Puppy Spot could not stop himself from moaning, though he might as well have taken it all with a full-throated sense of passion. After all, Mistress Steel had no interest in his pleasure and as soon as he had failed to satisfy her interest with one thing she moved on to something else. One moment the canine wasn't sure if he could hold back for a second more and the next he was left with a strained, lightly gaping, tail hole, lifted up and off her cock.

"Follow me, slave."

She stood, walking away without a second thought for him, disrobing herself of the strap-on. He whined and did not complain, following her on his knees, though it was a fight with every crawling motion to keep his attention away from his throbbing cock. It was easier not to cum when his tail hole wasn't being filled, though there was a big part of him that missed the stimulation of it, being filled and stretched out so devoutly.

Yet he was not there for himself but for her as the mare before him sat on the edge of the bed in the play room, setting up the lights above it so that all was illuminated in a soft, blue glow. He knew his place as he slipped between her legs and tenderly ran his tongue over her pussy, tugging her underwear to the side, of course, so that he had easy access. He only did not remove them because he had not been permitted to do so. And whatever Mistress Steel said or did not say was what he would follow.

Always hers. Always her obedient bitch.

For her domination was not solely to bring him pleasure, but to give them both what they needed. He settled into his place with a small smile on his face, one that Mistress Steel would never see, tongue dipping into her, curling and pulling, seeking out her G-spot only to drag back lustfully over it. No... He didn't need to orgasm to be satisfied, though the delicious denial of it left him squirming, his body still wanting it. He only needed to serve, his tail wagging back and forth lightly, focusing on her, only her.

"Deeper, slave..."

One more command as her hips bucked lustfully against him once again, driving him on to please her. Her tail hole was not left aside either as he ran his tongue passionately around it, even pushing inside, for the soft musk of her was far from unpleasant to him. It was all wrapped up in the scents and sweet textures of her body. And, in a way that he did not understand but did not have to either, pleasing her, his tongue dipping into her essence and drinking down everything she had to give him.

It did not take long, his tail hole gaping and his backside smarting, lust overwhelming. But Pup Spot was right there for Mistress Steel when she took her orgasm from him. Her hips rose fervently, grinding on to his nose while he helped her through her orgasm, ripples pulling around his tongue as he delved deep, using only his mouth and muzzle to please her.

Nothing else was needed, not as the tension and bond between them settled softly, closer than ever, her paw resting on his head, gently scratching his ear. It was the best kind of praise that he would get from her as he leaned gratefully into her touch, tongue swirling around her clit, dragging out the last vestiges of pleasure from her.

"You were always my favourite bitch…"

And that was all he needed. To be hers. To be used by her. To be her bitch. He smiled softly, resting his cheek against her inner thigh.

With Mistress Steel, he could never truly be denied.

Mistress of the Whip

Sweetheart, it is never that easy.

It is never that easy to bring a true male under your hand, wind his leash about your hand. And *pull* tight. The bois will break and whimper and grovel at your hooves, adoring them with kisses that never dig deeper than the surface. Perhaps a boi could be trained to bring you glasses of wine and paint your hooves a fierce scarlet, but that is about all the use there is for them. No, there is a much greater delight than holding a boi beneath a hard, unyielding hoof.

A zebra lady, such as myself, seeks the finer tastes of a male whose eyes bore into their soul, dominance challenging and tempers flaring. He may smirk. He is strong and he could overpower you in an instance, if he so chose. The difference is that, with you, he will not do this. You have him within your control, completely and utterly. In the end, that is. When it begins...a real male will *fight* you.

And it's your task to bring him down.

Living alone in a detached house, not too far out of town, may seem idyllic for some. My life was perfect to outside eyes, a zebra femfur living alone with plenty to entertain myself. The house had a lawn and a driveway and all the normal things, painfully normal, that one would expect from a femfur in her mid-thirties. I would not tell you my age, however – that would be uncouth. You do not ask that of a lady, did you not know? I possessed a good job in an office and was working my way up the career ladder. Pretty boring stuff when it comes right down to it, but it paid the bills and satisfied my tastes in the finer side of life, even if something was sorely missing.

Dating came less easily to me than my comfortable lifestyle when males realised I was disinclined to vanilla life. I had heard the word "freak" far more times than I can count, though that is no longer of any matter to me. Words bounce off when you have seen a wolf writhing in bondage, your strap-on cock driving into his backside while he begs for mercy. A new dating pool opened up to me and, despite not keeping the lads around for longer than it took to fulfil my needs, my sexuality sparked into a roaring fire.

I leaned back into my armchair with the curved back, crafted from dark brown leather that gleamed in the candlelight. How it shone so wonderfully was one of the reasons I had chosen it. The other was that it added to my aura of power. I liked that power.

My toy of the evening, a strapping young unicorn whose name I'd put to one side entered the room. He was my favourite breed: pale white with a spiralling, silver horn and a long, leonine tail with a thick drape of hair at the tip. His black hair was tousled although I had bid him to come looking presentable. Perhaps this was as presentable as this one came. That would have to change. He carried a silver tray – authentic, of course – with a single wine glass in the centre cradling ruby red wine. The liquid swilled back and forth in the glass as he clumsily stepped up to my chair, clacking his hooves and lowering himself to his knees with not an iota of grace. I smiled.

Sometimes, a little extra power went a long way.

Placing the tray on the side table beside my "throne," the unicorn lifted the wine glass to me, fingers curled around the bowl to offer me the stem. I took it delicately, eyes never leaving his. When he was broken in, his eyes would not come up from the ground without my permission, but the best ones always took time to break. There was beauty in the breaking and I was going to enjoy every second of his insolence before claiming him as mine.

"Will that be all?"

He stared me down, hazel eyes locked with mine as if he expected something more, that little quirk at the corner of his velvety, equine lips. He took in my attire, a corset and latex thong that left enough to the imagination that I could be anything he wanted me to be, if I so chose. Yet it was for him to please me, not the other way around. He had to be what I wanted him to be.

I adored the new ones, I really did. They came to me thinking that I was a zebra that would crumple at their hooves and gaze up at them with girlish eyes, eyelashes fluttering oh so sweetly. They were always so surprised, after all that, the build-up for months on end, when I was not so easy to break. I am not easy to break at all. Persistence will always come through trumps, they said, but it was yet to prove true for me.

I shook my head.

"You're forgetting something, unicorn."

He rolled his eyes and heaved a sigh, exaggerating the motion with a roll of his bare shoulders, rounded and muscled in testimony to all the time he undoubtedly spent pumping iron. It could have been a vain pursuit or a respectable one. Only time would tell as I slowly opened him up to me. The unicorn could be just like all the others who'd come before him.

"What am I forgetting?"

My lips curved into a wicked smile – one that I knew he would take as a challenge. Though he'd not done entirely badly so far, I'd give him that.

"Go clean up the kitchen," I directed, turning my eyes back to my book, left with a bookmark to denote my page on the side table. "You left the dishes in the sink from dinner. I want it as I left it before."

Though the order was simple – I wouldn't have given anything more complicated to one with his mind on his cock – the unicorn's lips twisted and both eyebrows shot dangerous high. His blatant disbelief was almost cute.

"Clean the kitchen?" He repeated, scoffing. "C'mon, we both know that's not what I'm really here for, you're just winding me up."

"I assure you that I am nothing but serious."

He shifted back on to the heels of his cloven hooves, though I was pleased to stay that he stayed on the floor at my hooves too. That was a good sign at least. Some – before him – had immediately jumped up and petulantly waved their arms about, making demands that I gave them what they had come for, what I apparently really wanted after all my games. They had tried to intimidate me. They had tried to get their way. They had failed.

"You have signed a contract for the night, boi." I felt my eyes narrowing just a fraction, though I didn't need to draw any more steel into my glare. "If you are invoking the clause to end our liaison, well... You can show yourself out."

He paused, eyes shifting between me and the door. I could have laughed at his helpless indecision. He was just like so many others, expecting a bona fide femdom experience where he was chained, bound and beaten – all for *his* pleasure, of course – and allowed to go home at the end of the night with his cock softening in his sheath, having spent himself so many times that one time more would be one time too many. And he hadn't found me up to his expectations. I didn't play around and I wasn't about to bend to the will of some wannabe submissive.

I sipped my wine, deliberately avoiding his stare. He'd have to get out of that bad habit too. No, I played for my pleasure and he had better learn that swiftly or else make good his escape. There were plenty more I could call on for pleasure.

Poor pony, too innocent for my touch. He wouldn't be getting off with me.

He turned on his heel, perhaps thinking his abrupt departure would alert me to his derision. Yet he left all the same and I knew he would be in there cleaning the dishes, even if he made more noise than was strictly necessary. My eyes slid to the clock on the wall. He did not take as long as most of the stubborn ones. I smiled. He would be a delight.

I seated myself more comfortably as the water ran in the kitchen, the unicorn finally putting himself to the task at hand. My wine commanded greater attention than he and I slowly, delectably drained the glass, sip by sip, as I allowed him more than adequate time to go about his work. Only when the last ruby droplets had slipped from the glass to my lips did I set the glass aside and rise, my sights set on the kitchen.

What greeted me was not a welcome one. He stood with his arms crossed, hoof tapping the smooth tiles as he threw his gaze between me and the dishes as if demanding acknowledgement of his accomplishment. Soap trickled down the plates and I inhaled slowly.

Did he think I would miss the scraps – tiny spots, really – of food still clinging to the plates? My meal from earlier had not been washed cleanly from their surface.

He tilted his horn cockily to the side as I shook mine, the grin not leaving his face. I smoothed my hand over my hip.

"Did you think this would be an adequate job?"

I frowned, hating to put such an expression on to my face when I was all made up for my pleasure. Yet he'd displeased me and his smug grin roused something fierce in the pit of my belly.

Rolling, his shoulders, the unicorn cast his eyes to the ceiling with a sigh that could have shaken the foundations of a kingdom.

"I didn't think I'd be coming out here to wash dishes," he said, flashing me what he probably thought was a winning grin. "I'm better than that. Better than all the others I'm sure you've had."

I raised an eyebrow.

"All the others?"

He blinked, taking half a step back. I hid my smile.

"I'm sure there have been others. Others wanting to come out to see you."

My expression did not change and the unicorn flinched, shuffling his hooves. His bare toes curled into the linoleum and he shivered, perhaps his nudity chill on his skin in the kitchen. But I did not care much for his comfort in that instance.

He sighed.

"What? Why are you just staring at me?"

"Because you haven't elaborated."

He scowled, handsome face twisting into something unseemly.

"You didn't ask me to elaborate."

I stilled, patiently watching and waiting as his discomfort grew. He could wince and shuffle as much as he liked though – I had all the time in the world.

"You have had others here, haven't you?" He said eventually, breaking the silence stretching between us. "You had the ad on the forum. You wanted people to come here. You were looking for people just like me..." He hesitated. "Weren't you?"

I pursed my lips, just enough for him to notice.

"What makes you think there were many of them?"

He laughed at that, throwing his head back as his cocky smile returned.

"Someone only has to look at your photos up there to see what a slut you are, Harriet. They're plastered all over the place. It couldn't be more fucking obvious that all you're really looking for is to get your cunt filled."

I inhaled sharply, nostrils flaring. Yet it was nothing I hadn't heard before. It was what they liked to assume, after all.

"You don't get to use my name tonight. I am Mistress to you and that title alone."

He smirked.

"And what exactly are you going to do about that?" He rolled his shoulders and yawned, stretching and flexing the muscles in his arms. "Can't we just get to the chase and get you on all fours already, tail flagged for me? I'm sick of these games. It's all going to the same place anyway and I don't know why you insist on playing these games."

I smiled, hiding my fury behind painted lips. That little unicorn didn't know what he was playing with.

"Why did you take the time to sign my contract if you didn't like playing games?"

He snorted.

"Not as if I took the fucking time to read it. It's not going to be binding."

"Yet anything I do to you that's contained in that contract will be regarded as consensual." I lifted a hand, my smile too innocent to be believed. "If you believe you'll be screwing me on all fours tonight, you are incorrect. So very incorrect."

My words, so formal, slipped sinuously from my tongue, practiced. It was not as if they had not passed my lips before. The bois were no different, all wanting the same thing these days and expecting to get it with minimal effort.

I pressed on.

"But if you want the treatment that will pleasure both you and I, then you may be in for something a shade more desirable, my sweet."

I caressed his face, running just my finger up the line of his jaw to his lips. He trembled, eyes fixed on mine. I was impressed by how they did not drop to my breasts, not even once throughout my whole little speech.

I grabbed his face, holding his stare unblinkingly. He flinched, but I would not release him, painted fingernails digging into his chin.

"I am not for you. You are for me. Get that into your thick stallion skull and maybe we'll get along here. Or else you can leave. Trot out right now, if you're not prepared to give me exactly what *I* want and forget your own pathetic desires."

He cast his eyes down, smirk twisting into a stubborn frown. But the reaction of his body told me all I needed to know. I pushed him away, letting him stumble back half a pace as his cock rose from his bare sheath, swelling with blood. Of course, I had not allowed him any clothes. He didn't deserve clothes in my presence.

I snapped my fingers. I had him, I knew I did. But I couldn't let him know that I knew.

"Follow."

Turning on my heel, I strode from the kitchen, pacing straight through the room where I had seated myself previously. I had something far better in mind than what play could be had in there.

To my surprise and subtle pride, he followed me without a word until I paused in the doorway, a slip of black fabric in my hands. He eyed it distrustfully and I raised and eased it over his head without a word. It scooted down over his eyes, its function clear: a blindfold. He shivered, the tremble running through his body and down the length of his cock. I smiled, out of his sight. I was confident it was achingly hard. Just for me. All for me.

Only not quite in the way he expected.

"You have much to learn, little one," I whispered, following up the blindfold with a cool circle of latex around his throat, buckling it neatly at the back of his neck and brushing his mane aside. "And I will be there to teach you every step of the way. All you have to do is give yourself to me, completely and utterly."

He reached up to touch the latex, though I couldn't help but notice the tremble in his fingertips.

"What is this?"

"I don't recall asking you to speak. Must I gag you? Your moans will be delightful and I would hate to quell them so."

He froze, pulse fluttering at the base of his throat.

"Since you should know, this once... That around your neck, unicorn, is a collar. A latex one."

I trailed my hand down his toned chest and stomach, stopping short of his crotch. His lips parted, but he held his words back, cock twitching as it pulsed with blood.

Excellent. He was learning.

Clipping a chain leash to the collar, I jingled it lightly, letting him hear. He started, head jerking up higher.

"Come now. Follow me."

Leading him into part of the house that he had not yet had the privilege to see, I took him upstairs, his steps faltering as he turned his head from left to right. He did not reach with his hands to balance himself, instead trying to take each step with the feel of his hooves alone. Easing over smooth carpet, I let him take his time, keeping only enough tension in the chain leash to let him know I was there.

"Mistress?" He whispered, head ducked as he looked for steps he could not see. "I... What if I fall?"

Pausing halfway up the stairs, I rested my hand on his chest, fingers splayed so that they grazed his collarbone.

"You'll simply have to trust me. Come on now."

I encouraged him on and, in no time at all, we found ourselves at the top of the stairs. He stumbled, expecting another step, but I let him find his own balance again. He'd have to keep himself balanced in a much more precarious situation, after all. This was only practice – a reminder of our differing status.

Leading him into what he would later learn was my play room, I dropped the leash, leaving him in the centre of the room with no sense of direction. He turned his head, seeking bearings that would not come, as I circled him, hooves rapping over the floor. I shivered, taking a moment for my own, delicious pleasure. I adored that sound.

And he would be everything I needed, even if he did not know it at the moment. A firm body, rolling with muscle... Oh, it had been so long since I'd had one as fine as him in body, a spirit primed for breaking. As fun as he would be to play with, however, he would have to be punished for his earlier transgressions. Something in the rise and fall of his chest, on the other hand, told me it would be exactly the brand of humiliation he craved.

"Arms above your head, pony."

He made a face, but did as told, turning his head from side to side once again as if he could see through the blindfold as if he tried hard enough. He'd soon give up on that though.

"Good...good..."

Grasping the chain hanging from the ceiling, I let it lower to his raised wrists, bumping lightly against palms and fingertips in a metal kiss. He spread his hooves further apart, swaying even though I had not attached him to the chain as yet. I smiled. He reacted just as I thought he would, pushing towards the true object of his desire.

I ran my hand down his back, latex cuffs tucked neatly into my other palm where he would not see or feel them.

"For now, you have a latex collar, boi. Do you know why that is?"

He shook his head, lips pressed firmly together.

"It is because you have not yet earned my leather collar, impatient pony."

I circled him again, hooves clicking rhythmically. Pausing in front of him, I studied the lines of his face, lips parted as if to take my lips up against his own. But those would not be the kind of kisses he'd be getting from me.

"If you wish for my collar, my ownership, you shall have to earn it. You must prove your servitude and, yes, your love. It is not my place to tell you how to do that. That would be spoon feeding you and, frankly, I don't have the time to educate a submissive in how to be submissive. You've claimed, quite ostentatiously, I may add, that you are the best of the best already."

He flinched and I laughed, latching the latex cuffs around his wrists and securing them tightly with the buckles away from curious fingertips. With the cuffs locked together, palm to palm, there would be no way he'd get out of them, not with what I had in mind.

"Ah, did you not think I'd read your profile? It's up there for all to see. I do my research too. I look at your pictures before choosing my next one, my trial run sub, so to speak. There's plenty of options."

Pulling the chain down, I pushed it through the O-ring on the cuffs and linked it back up with itself, securing his arms above his head with a little leeway. He'd probably need that inch or two of slack, though it could be tightened if I so chose.

He sucked in a breath, chest heaving as they came quicker, as if he was not quite able to get enough air into his lungs. I pressed my fingers fleetingly to his vulnerable, arched neck, delighting in the flicker of his pulse against my fingertips, so beautiful in its pace.

"Ah, you like the thought of that, don't you?" I teased. "You like the thought of your mistress vetting you and choosing the for her playtime, her household. You are as clear to read as my own reflection in the mirror and as familiar as such too."

He groaned and shook his head, though there was no conviction in the motion. His forehead shone, nervous sweat glistening on his skin.

"If you do not wish for my collar, we may have one night together and go on our way," I continued, stepping back to observe my work. "One night of pleasure and one night to remember."

I shrugged, fingers on his blindfold, slipping it from the unicorn's fine face.

"I shall have many more to try, if you fail like those gone before you."

He blinked, adjusting to the dimmer light of my play room after his own world of darkness. And what he saw made him reel, eyes widening in shock. His cock throbbed, a drop of pre cum gleaming at the tip. I saw it. He had eyes for too much else to take note of the condition of his own body.

My play room was a masterpiece. Clad in black and red – traditional and cliché, I know, but it was *my* room to design as I wanted it, precisely so – it contained every manner of play equipment that I had, so far, been able to source. A cross stood on one side of the room, proudly dangling manacles – lockable, of course. Opposite was a long shelf that ran the full length of the room, filled with dildos of varying shapes and sizes, organised by size and girth. I was precise in my organisation, I had been told, but who wanted to hunt through chests and boxes in the middle of a play session? At least I knew where everything was.

A polished oak spanking bench stood a few paces before my partner and he eyed it hungrily, eyes drinking in the sheen of the gleaming wood. A paddle lay beside it, on one of the knee rests, just in case I wanted to reach for it quickly. It had come in useful many times and it did make such a beautiful noise as it whistled through the air, only the highest quality and the largest price tag for my collection. The crack spoke of even higher figures, the finest craftsmanship money could buy as it turned a submissive unicorn's backside black and blue for days on end.

I took a moment to survey my collection, not without a subtle murmur of shared pleasure. Money certainly did buy me some happiness. Though not all of it. Some happiness could only come from companionship. Yet it had to be the right kind of companionship and, truly, there were so many different kinds, for me, that could not be satisfied by laughter and friendship.

I sighed, hiding the rise and fall of my breasts from him. Would he be the one I'd been looking for all this time? He gulped, eyes on my wall of whips, every implement that I could lay my hands on proudly displayed for my play partners to see. I murmured appreciatively. He was certainly heading in the right direction, that much was sure.

"I see something has caught your attention."

I paced to the wall, casting my gaze over the myriad of whips that seemed to have commanded his attention.

"Was it this one? Or this, perhaps?" I rested my hand on a short cane, usually used for showing horses. "This does make a wonderful crack when it hits. I don't need to put my full arm into it either, though it raises welts for days. Even through fur – and you don't have much to protect your ass."

I smirked powerfully, memory lacing my smile.

"My last pet, the last one I used this one on..." I took it from the wall and ran my fingers over it, enjoying the feel of stretched leather over the implement, so innocent yet vicious. "Well, let me simply say that he did not sit down properly for days afterwards. He told me so. And sent me the photos to prove it."

He baulked, taking a step back as the chain clinked above his head. I grinned, teeth flashing white.

"It shall make an excellent first implement for you. I do hope you enjoy how it *sings*."

Tapping the cane against my palm, I selected two more, hiding them behind my back and placing them carefully out of his line of sight as I joined him once again. He gulped visibly and shook his head, though did not allow a word to pass his lips.

"Such beauty in how you hold yourself," I murmured, placing the tip of the cane beneath his swollen cock, which had not softened even a little with a pleasingly raised medial ring. "You want this."

I met his gaze.

"Remember your safe word, little one."

He struggled, eyes wide, as I stood behind him and brought my arm back, not allowing him any build up or warning. The crack of it on his skin would be build up enough as I brought a red flush to his buttocks. With his white hair, I'd likely see a glow of it, even when I could not enjoy quite as much with other playthings of mine.

I chuckled wickedly as I brought it down, loving my laugh as much as the almighty crack that resounded through the room. He shrieked, shooting up on to his toes as the blow landed, anticipating the pain before it had actually struck. When it registered, his eyes bulged and he danced from hoof to hoof, a howl ripping itself from his lips. I did not pause – letting the pain set in and linger would be worse – and brought the cane down twice more in quick succession, scoring two more red lines across his muscled backside.

Squealing like a pig, he bounced back and forth, swinging and yelling when the chain caught his weight, hooves scraping for balance that would not come. I shook my head. I hadn't even hit that hard. Was it really his first time tasting the lick of an impact tool on his rear? Surely not.

Whimpering pathetically – even I thought so, though it sent a shiver down my spine – he dropped his head, something falling from his eye to the floor. I stiffened. Tears? He was crying?

How disappointing.

"Do you need to stop?" I frowned, passing the whip to my other hand. "Are you going to displease me so swiftly?"

I faked a sigh, though he would not have known that it was anything but genuine.

"What a pity. And I had such high hopes..."

"No! Mistress!"

He craned his head about, shifting from hoof to hoof as the chain took more of his weight, shoulders twisting around. His eyes were wild, moisture glistening in the corners, as his dark hair clung to the arch of his neck, slick with darkening patches of sweat.

"I don't want to stop, Mistress – please!" He ground his teeth together, jaw working. "I can do this! I don't want to use my safe word!"

"So, what are you saying...slut?" I pressed, running the cane over the rising welts I'd created – he winced. "Is this what you want? Is this what you need? Far more than getting a femfur on all fours and fucking her, as you so crudely put it to me?"

He hung his head.

"I'm sorry, Mistress, I was wrong." He screwed up his pretty face as if it pained him to let the words pass his lips. "I was wrong, I was thinking of myself..." He stared at the floor, unblinking. "I wasn't thinking of you when that's all I should have been thinking of. I'm sorry, Mistress."

I cupped his chin gently but did not make him look me in the eyes, letting him devour my body with his gaze instead – a small reward for good behaviour.

"Then you shall please me further, pony. But your breaking has only just begun."

I cracked the cane on his ass again, laughing at his shriek and how his tail lashed, even if it could not protect him. I could rest sure in my heart that he knew he could stop it at any point, but his determination to keep going raised my respect for him. He wanted to please me, even if he was clearly unused to my level of pain. That, above all else, showed that he wanted to please me. And I *liked* that.

Only when I had covered his backside in a series of thick welts and his chest heaved did I put the cane aside, letting it clatter to the floor. He'd tidy them up later for me. He dragged his head around, exhaustion lining his body after only a few minutes of beating. But pain would do that to a person. His cock had softened, but, at the release of pain, swelled with blood once more, eyes shining with what I liked to think was a growing devotion to me and me alone.

"This one..." I smiled, selecting my next whip. "This one is my favourite."

I held it up for him, a riding crop clasped between a thumb and finger. The black length thrummed as he sucked in a breath, eyes wide and starting. The triangular flap on the end would not be as vicious as the cane, but he was not to know that.

"Try to scream for me again, won't you?" I winked. "I did so love that sound. It was most pleasing to me, little one."

The pony tensed before the whip touched his skin and I whipped it back, arm further away from his body than it had needed to be for the cane. I cracked it across each cheek – one each – and smiled at his shriek, gritting his teeth to cut it off as if he did not actually want me to hear him cry out so. Perhaps he did not want me to think him weak? I liked that thought too. That thought made the heat in my crotch grow, dampness sliding over my thong – my favourite latex one. It would be gleaming with my own arousal by the time we were good and done in the play room.

Taking the crop more easily than he had the cane – better to start with a harsh one to let them know what they were really up against, really – the unicorn held his breath through a flurry of strokes, legs trembling. He spread his hooves apart for balance and closed his eyes, holding himself firm through the strokes even as they came down on his existing welts. Though he shuddered forward, he did not collapse into the chains again, sweat rolling down his back from the base of his neck and shoulder blades.

But I couldn't allow him to become too used to the strokes and, well, a mistress had her ways to keep a submissive on their toes, it had to be said. Cracking the whip down on the worst of his welts, I fed fresh fire to his existing pain, coaxing a howl from his lips as he pushed back up on to his toes. Even as his body strove to dance away from my touch, I grabbed his hip and forced him back into place, swinging the crop up with, thankfully for him, less force. It sailed up and between his legs to tap into his balls, a square strike with the flap at the tip of the crop.

Although the blow was lighter – far lighter than the strikes I'd been raining down on his backside – he shot up and into the chains. They caught and pulled him back as he sucked in breath, only to be expelled a moment later in the most beautiful of screams. Chuckling, I released him, allowing him to find his own footing again, but not without a second tap to his precious orbs, lighter this time. He squealed just as beautifully and danced, trying to close his legs but finding that he could not shudder away from the pain while keeping his nuts suitably protected.

It was a vicious choice and he played it out wonderfully for me as I teasingly struck his ass throughout it all, reminding him exactly who was in control. Whenever he thought he had the upper hand, he never would: it would always, irrevocably, be me, above all else.

"You are beautiful," I whispered, knowing my words would carry.

He groaned and let his weight fall into the chains, legs trembling. I ran the whip softly over my palm, a gentler kiss than the ones I'd given him. It was time for the finale, at least for what I had planned to get my submissive in line.

The bullwhip was my final toy, though it was difficult to see it as something sexual when one considered the raw power behind it. The well-oiled and maintained leather slid between my fingers as I played with the five-foot length, holding back my moan. Just touching it made my pussy wetter, though that pleasure would soon come – I only had to be patient. It was always better to wait, after all, to wind myself up tighter and tighter until I was as taut as possible, body balanced on the pinnacle of release before I'd even touched my clit.

Whipping made me a sadist, yet it was my pets that made me love it so.

"Remember your safe word."

His head shot around as I brought my arm up in front of me, taking a step back to allow the whip room to sail out to its full length. Flicking it back, I pulled power into the leather and cracked it out, tip scoring a line across his upper back.

Perfect.

He squealed, though the pain, I knew, was more of a sting than a deeper burn. Yet I could be confident that he had never been whipped there, much less anywhere for any extended period of time. To my interest, the stallion's cock did not soften this time, but hardened, dripping more and more pre cum. Licking my lips, I ached to scoop it on to my finger and press it into his mouth, forcing him to taste the essence of himself.

"Please, Mistress..." He whispered hoarsely, shoulders pulled back. "Please...no more..."

"Are you using your safe word?"

He shut his mouth, eyes closed, and said no more.

The bullwhip sang out, tip cracking, but I only played it an inch from his buttocks, making him jump. Sometimes the anticipation of a hit was as potent as the strike itself – far more so than the fear of a cane or crop could ever have been. I layered the whip lovingly over his back and buttocks, watching the red lines grow and grow until he was criss-crossed with them. Every time the time lanced over a welt, he squealed and jumped, bouncing until the pain subsided until the slow, dull throb that I wagered he was becoming used to, bit by bit. There would only be more if he ever did become completely used to it.

I smiled. Already the unicorn craved all I had to give. When my next stroke with the bullwhip did not come immediately, he pushed his buttocks back, muscles shuddering. I rewarded him for that by allowing the tip of the whip to wrap around the side of his hip as it hit, speeding up as the body of it made impact before the tip. He sucked in a breath and gasped, eyes wide. Sweat dripped off his arms and back, droplets of it flying off the whip as I sent it out again and again, drawing him to the very limit of what his body was able to endure.

On the hardest strikes, his cock softened, but always came back to full mast when I let off, much to my pleasure. But there was only so much a boi could take and mine was tired, oh so very tired, after his first taste of my whip and bite of pain.

Tossing the bullwhip aside – I missed the feel of its handle seated in my palm already – I pressed the length of my body against the unicorn's back. Rather than leaning into my breasts, as he might have done upon first arriving in my home, he groaned and stood perfectly still, trembling as I explored his body with my hands and drew a fresh rise of pain from his bruises and welts. He cried out softly, barely enough breath left in his lungs to voice any complaint, and submitted to my touch.

"That was your punishment for displeasing me, pony," I whispered, breath tickling his ear. "I'd say that you're never going to do it again, not if you receive this treatment, but there's a part of you that loves this, isn't there? You want pain. You crave it. You *need* it."

He whimpered and shook his head, eyes cast down to the floor. But I knew the truth.

"Expect me to find another punishment if you displease me again. I need not use my single arrow from my quiver over and over again with whoever I take. Do you understand that?"

Nodding quickly, he barked an answer, eyes wide and strained.

"Yes, Mistress!"

"Excellent."

Reaching around his stomach, I wrapped my fingers around his nicely thick shaft, smiling at the weight of it pressing down on my palm. He wouldn't have won any size contests against real stallions, that was for sure, but it was a good size, a size that pleased me. This time he did push into my touch, hips jerking up of their own accord as I pumped my hand along his length.

"Do you think you've earned this?" I hissed through my teeth, stroking his cock with the lightest of touches. "Do you think you've earned the right to cum in my presence?"

Pleasure mingled with pain and he twisted back and forth, body at my whim to do with as I pleased, completely and utterly. But I was waiting for an answer and pulled my hand from his cock, letting him buck and thrust into midair, with no further stimulation forthcoming. Howling, he shook his head, dark hair flying where it had not stuck to his skin.

"No, Mistress!" He yelped, words seeming thick and heavy to force out of his mouth. "I haven't earned it! I haven't earned the right to cum with you, I haven't!"

He stopped trying to thrust, forcing his hips still as he pressed his hooves flat to the floor. A new determination entered his eyes as I pushed my chin over his shoulder – I could do with him as I wanted, after all, and his space was mine to invade – studying him.

"I am yours to do with as you will," he said after a long pause that stretched out and out and out, drawing in a shuddering breath. "But I don't need to tell you that. You know it already. You just want to make me say it. You want to hear it...from me."

I smiled.

"Then you understand, little one."

I pushed away, unlocking the cuffs holding his wrists up to the chain with a deft flick of my fingers. He swayed and crumpled to the floor, knees hitting the hard surface first as he worked out the soreness from his arms. Looking down at his cock, he moved as if to touch it, but steadied himself, letting his hands fall back to his sides.

Good pony.

I smiled and he blinked, hope brightening his features and overshadowing the flicker of doubt there. Poor unicorn. Good unicorn. He'd done well, for his first time. I hadn't even beaten him for very long, truth be told. Yet there would be no release for him, not this time. Myself, on the other hand...

The pony spread his knees, trying to keep his buttocks off his legs as I stalked him, one hand grasping his mane. I had not paid too much attention to my attire for the evening – anything would have been spectacular, I was sure – but a corset and latex thong combination did come in very useful. The corset didn't even need to be laced particularly tightly for the effect I desired. And the desire in his eyes brought fresh fire to mine. I licked my lips.

"Now, little one..."

I lifted my leg, slipping it over his shoulder to bring my pussy up to his face. My latex thong was easily tugged aside to press my dark, slick pussy lips to his face. He groaned, trembling closer as he parted his lips, hesitating in the moment. He looked up me, eyes wide and pleading, wordlessly asking for permission to take what he so desperately wanted. I smiled and nodded, grabbing a handful of his mane to drag him in closer.

"It is time for you to make good on your contract."

Inhaling sharply, he looked up at me, squirming as he sat too far back, pressing on his abused rear. Whimpering, he shot up and pushed his face into my pussy, sucking in my scent in greedy, short breaths, tongue flicking out the same time I gave the breathless command that would begin the rest of our night together.

"Lick."

Thank you for reading and I hope that everything was very much enjoyed!

Ready for more? Check out my author website for more furry fiction and where you can purchase my books!

https://linktr.ee/amethystmare

Cover art illustrated by verysweetpotato; they are contactable via Twitter for work enquiries.

twitter.com/AlexandrCorvin